IDEA S

INSTITUTE FOR JEWISH
IDEAS AND IDEALS

Presented by
John and Marjory Lewin

in honor of

Rabbi Marc and Gilda Angel

Congregation Shearith Israel Dinner
April 6, 2008

8 WEST 70TH STREET   NEW YORK NY 10023   WWW.JEWISHIDEAS.ORG

THE SEARCH COMMITTEE

THE SEARCH COMMITTEE

A NOVEL

MARC ANGEL

URIM FICTION

Jerusalem • New York

The Search Committee: A Novel
by Marc Angel
Copyright © 2008 by Marc D. Angel

Printed in Israel. First Edition. Layout design by Satya Levine.
ISBN 978-965-524-012-2

URIM FICTION
Urim Publications, P.O. Box 52287, Jerusalem 91521 Israel
Lambda Publishers Inc.
527 Empire Blvd., Brooklyn, New York 11225 U.S.A.
Tel: 718-972-5449 Fax: 718-972-6307 mh@ejudaica.com
www.UrimPublications.com

THE SEARCH COMMITTEE

Sunday, 9:00 a.m.
RAV SHIMSHON GROSSMAN [9]

Sunday, 2:00 p.m.
RAV DAVID MERCADO [23]

Monday, 9:00 a.m.
MRS. DEENA LEAH GROSSMAN [40]

Monday, 7:00 p.m.
MRS. SULTANA MERCADO [50]

Tuesday, 9:00 a.m.
RABBI SHABSAI VELT [69]

Tuesday, 7:00 p.m.
RAV HAZKEL GOTTLIEB [82]

Wednesday, 9:00 a.m.
SHAMMAI ABELSON [90]

Wednesday, 12:00 Noon
CHAIM BARUCH HABER [101]

Thursday, 9:00 a.m.
MR. CLYDE ROBINSON [114]

Thursday, 7:00 p.m.
MRS. ESTHER NEUHAUS [129]

Friday, 9:00 a.m.
MR. GERSHOM LYON [140]

Sunday, 9:00 a.m.
RAV SHIMSHON GROSSMAN [144]

Sunday, 11:00 a.m.
RABBI DAVID MERCADO [151]

Rav Shimshon Grossman

MEMBERS OF THE SEARCH COMMITTEE: I must confess my surprise that this meeting has been scheduled. I was under the impression that the appointment of the next rosh yeshiva, the head of our Torah academy, was simply a matter of formality. I had assumed, and still do assume, that I am the natural successor to this office.

You all know that our institution, Yeshivas Lita, was founded nearly fifty years ago by my grandfather, Rabbi Leibel Grossman, may the memory of the righteous be a blessing. Rav Leibel was born and raised among the finest Torah scholars of Europe and was privileged to study in the great yeshivas of Brisk and Volozhin. He had been teaching Talmud in the yeshiva of Berlin when Hitler, may his name be blotted out, came to power. Rav Leibel was quick to recognize the coming tragedy for European Jewry. He hastily mobilized his family and some students, and they managed to obtain the necessary papers for entry into the United States. His entourage arrived in New York in 1934.

When Rav Leibel settled here, he was already a renowned scholar. A number of learned and prosperous individuals in New York immediately came to his assistance. "Tell us what you want, Rav Leibel, and we will do our best to help you." Rav Leibel had one answer: "I want to establish a great yeshiva here in America, in the tradition of the famous yeshivos of Eastern Europe."

With the help of supporters and with tireless self-sacrifice, Rav Leibel opened Yeshivas Lita in August 1938. As European Jewry was about to be reduced to ashes by the accursed Nazis and their collaborators – may the Almighty wreak vengeance on their souls – a new light of Torah began to shine in America.

Yeshivas Lita attracted the best and the brightest young men of the Torah community. Rav Leibel's rigorous intellect and his prodigious knowledge were widely recognized. Our yeshiva grew steadily and soon became the premier yeshiva of advanced Talmudic study in the country.

Sadly, as you know, Rav Leibel died suddenly in the summer of 1945. The doctors said it was a heart attack. But our family tradition is that he actually died of a broken heart. The war years in Europe had a catastrophic impact on the Jews – millions of men, women and children were viciously murdered by our enemies and the enemies of God. Among the victims were many members of Rav Leibel's family – his students, his colleagues, his friends. He tormented himself that he was in New York, studying and teaching Torah in freedom, while so many of his loved ones were being butchered by the savage hordes of Christian Europe. He worked feverishly to find ways of helping Jews to escape from Europe and to help those refugees who arrived in America. He brought a number of young refugee men into our yeshiva and provided them with room and board as well as free schooling.

But he was crushed by the weight of the tragedy that befell our people. If a few were saved from the fires of Europe, millions were not.

He grieved and mourned. In spite of the success of Yeshivas Lita in New York, Rav Leibel's soul was bound to the souls of his brothers and sisters in Europe. When they were dying, he knew that he was dying. By the time the war was coming to an end, Rav Leibel knew that his life was coming to an end. When he died, he was another of Hitler's victims. The doctors said it was a heart attack. It was not a heart attack: it was a broken heart.

Upon Rav Leibel's death, my father – who was then only thirty years old – was immediately appointed as rosh yeshiva in place of my grandfather. I am sure the yeshiva did not commission a search committee then! No, of course not. It was natural that my father should succeed my grandfather. Who would have dared imagine otherwise?

My father, Rav Yosef Grossman, peace be upon his soul, was our rosh yeshiva for nearly forty years until his death. All of you knew him. He followed in the tradition of Rav Leibel, attracting many students, gaining many supporters. His commentaries on Maimonides's *Code of Jewish Law* are modern-day classics in the Torah world.

During his tenure as rosh yeshiva from 1945 to 1985, my father Rav Yosef devoted himself, heart and soul, to this institution. For him, Yeshivas Lita was a memorial not just to his father, but to all the Jews who were murdered in the Holocaust in Europe. When he began in 1945, we had perhaps one hundred and twenty-five students. The yeshiva consisted of one classroom building that also had some space designated as a dormitory. When he passed on in 1985, the yeshiva had grown to include the original classroom building, a *Beis Medrash,* and two new dormitories. Our enrollment had gone up to nearly six hundred students. In 1945, all the classes were taught by my father and a faculty of four rebbeim. In 1985, we had a faculty of twenty-five. As the yeshiva grew, I remember my father wondering how all the bills would be paid. He used to say: "Rich or poor, it's good to have money!"

Although he spent most of his days and nights studying and teaching Torah, he somehow also found time to cultivate followers among the laymen of the community. He gained their respect, taught them Torah lessons on their level, and encouraged them to contribute to the maintenance of Yeshivas Lita. All of you on the committee are here because my father, of blessed memory, invited you to become involved in the management and support of the yeshiva.

My parents, of blessed memory, had five children – myself and my four sisters. As the only son in our family, I began Torah study at an early age. I did not go to school, but rather learned entirely under my father's tutelage and under the tutors he hired for me. I entered Yeshivas Lita in August 1955 – when I was only thirteen – although most of the other students were at least seventeen or eighteen years old. I was precocious, hard-working and devoted to my father, so I succeeded in my studies. "For they" – the words of Torah – "are our life and the length of our days, and on them shall we meditate day and night." This was my motto.

Members of the Search Committee, you have asked me to address several questions. First, you want me to explain why I believe myself qualified to become the rosh yeshiva.

I do not know whether to treat this question as an expression of a strange sense of humor, or as a simple insult, an outrage. At this point in my life, I do not think I need to be called upon to explain my qualifications. They should be self-evident. You have all known me for many years; some of you have known me all my life.

When my father died, it was universally assumed that I would succeed him, just as he succeeded his father. Yet, nearly a year has passed, and no formal appointment has been made. Frankly, I am perplexed by the delay. I know that the committee wishes to appear to be open and democratic, to go through the charade of a search. But that is your problem; it should not be mine. You simply should have met for a brief meeting, and decided on the spot that I was to be the new rosh yeshiva. That you have actually invited me to appear before you to justify myself – this borders on the ridiculous!

Who are you to stand in judgment of my qualifications? Are you learned talmudists, Torah scholars? Not by a long way! What are your qualifications, Members of the Search Committee, to merit the responsibility of selecting a rosh yeshiva? You have none! You are well-intentioned people, I trust. You are supporters of the yeshiva. You are on the committee either because you are a major contributor to Yeshivas Lita or because you have rendered some extraordinary service to it. But you do not have – and do not claim to have – a high degree of Torah knowledge. Woe unto our community when Torah positions are determined by prominent individuals who, with all due respect, are ignorant of the complexities of Torah.

I do not mean to insult you. But neither do I wish to be insulted. The honor of the Torah is precious to me.

However, since you have insisted that I list my qualifications, I will defer to you. I do not wish to be on bad terms with you; I wish to work with you for many years to come for the benefit of our yeshiva.

My first qualification, as I have already described, is my *yichus,* my family pedigree. My grandfather and my father both served as the rosh yeshiva of Yeshivas Lita; I would be the third link in the chain. "The three-stranded rope does not quickly unravel." Our faculty, students and supporters all expect me to be the rosh yeshiva, since I have been bred from infancy to become the rosh yeshiva. I symbolize in my very person all the history and traditions of this yeshiva. I am identified with Yeshivas Lita as no other human being can be.

As you know, a rosh yeshiva cannot rest only on the laurels of his distinguished ancestors and teachers. He must be a world-class, widely-recognized Torah authority. It pains my sense of humility to have to speak of my own stature as a Torah scholar. My father ordained me when I was only twenty years old. He assigned me to teach the Talmud class to the incoming students, who were just a few years younger than I. As the years went on, my father assigned me to higher-level classes. For the past ten years I have been teaching the top-level class, and have recommended to my father which students should be ordained and which should not.

The other Talmud teachers – with one or two exceptions – have looked to me as the leading scholar of our institution – after my father, that is. With my father's passing, they naturally defer to me. So this is my third qualification: I am held in high esteem by faculty and students. They listen to me. They accept my authority. They turn to me for guidance in all matters of Torah scholarship and rabbinic law. Although I am reluctant to use the phrase, many people consider me to be the *gadol ha-dor,* the greatest Torah giant of this generation.

You asked me to respond to another question: what is my vision for the future of Yeshivas Lita?

My answer is simple: let us walk in the ways of our fathers, veering neither to the right nor to the left. Let us be faithful to our mission: teaching Talmud on the highest level, in the tradition of the now-defunct yeshivos of Lithuania and Poland. We demand intellectual rigor, razor-sharp analysis, tireless devotion to learning Torah for its own sake.

Our yeshiva is an island of purity in a filthy and immoral world. We want to protect our students, insulate them from the temptations and vulgarities of America's hedonism and materialism. We want to raise a generation of upright Torah scholars who live for Torah and nothing but Torah.

Let us not be deceived: the outside world is a spiritual cesspool. The arts and literature of modern America are decadent. Sexual promiscuity is the norm. The virtues of holiness and modesty are entirely absent from the popular mass culture of society. Everything is money, sex, power. The average American cares much more about the stock market than about God. The average American cares much more about baseball than about God!

Yeshivas Lita is an institution dedicated entirely to training young men to live in God's ways. Through study and prayer, through fulfillment of the commandments of the Torah, we attempt to create an ideal society. We shut out the pollution of the world; we immerse ourselves in the purity of Torah.

The Talmud tells the story of Rabbi Yosei ben Kisma. A man approached him and asked: "Rabbi, from what town are you?" Rabbi Yosei ben Kisma answered: "I am from a town of great Torah sages." You notice: he did not give the name of his town, but he gave a description of its spiritual quality. This is, after all, what is truly important in life. The man, obviously impressed with Rabbi Yosei, offered him a tremendous sum of money if he would leave his town and come to serve the man's community as their rabbi. Rabbi Yosei replied: If you were to offer me all the money in the world, I would not live anywhere except in a place filled with Torah scholars.

Rabbi Yosei ben Kisma was giving us a model, an ideal. He was teaching us that the most important thing for us is to live in a society dedicated to Torah learning. All the money in the world would not distract him from this ideal, and no material concerns should distract us from this ideal.

Yeshivas Lita exists to educate young Torah scholars in an environment totally imbued with Torah scholarship and Torah living. We hope to inspire them to devote their lives to Torah – studying, teaching, strengthening the Torah community. We want to immunize them from the corruption and materialism of the outside world. The deeper they plunge themselves into the sea of Torah study, the greater freedom and inner strength they will attain.

Thank the Lord, many of our students of past years have gone on to become teachers and role models in their communities. Individual by individual, family by family, neighborhood by neighborhood – our yeshiva has been changing the face of American Jewry. While so many of our co-religionists have abandoned Torah and halakha, the graduates of our yeshiva have been bringing hundreds of Jews back to the wellsprings of their religious tradition.

My vision for the future is: let us renew our days as the days of old. Let us keep our eyes focused on the achievements of our predecessors, and let us walk in their ways.

I stand before you as a man who grew up in this yeshiva, who was nurtured by its environment, who has ever been loyal to its traditions. I love the yeshiva as I love life itself. I was young, and now I have grown older. The sandy hair of my youth has turned gray; the smooth face of my childhood has given way to a long beard. But I am still the same person inside, with the same fire and the same vision.

Members of the Search Committee, you have asked me to respond to one more question: why do I think I am the best candidate for the position of rosh yeshiva?

This is a most perplexing question. You apparently want me to compare myself to other possible candidates, and to point out why I am better and they are worse. This borders on the sin of gossip and slander. I have told you my virtues, and that should suffice. But you are not satisfied to know my qualifications. You also want to know why I am the "best" candidate. This assumes that you have other candidates, or at least another candidate, in mind. As you may imagine, I find this astounding. In fact, I cannot even think of another qualified candidate, let alone one who is more qualified than I am.

I am the senior Talmud teacher in our yeshiva. None of the other teachers would presume to become rosh yeshiva over my head. They all know their place. And I cannot think of any Torah scholar from outside our yeshiva who would be more suitable to serve as our rosh yeshiva than I.

I have heard some whisperings that one or two of you are favorable to one of our Talmud instructors, Rabbi David Mercado. When I first heard these whispers, I was amazed beyond words. Surely, such an idea is too ludicrous to be taken seriously. Mercado is an outsider, a relative newcomer to our yeshiva. Yes, he has been teaching here for some years, yet he has never really integrated himself into the yeshiva's culture. When my father, of blessed memory, decided to hire Mercado as an instructor of Talmud, I objected strenuously. I told my father: This fellow is a flashy show-off, a fake. He pretends to know a lot, but he really knows very little. He spends more time studying secular books than he does poring over the pages of Talmud. He is contaminated by strange and foreign ideas. He can't be trusted. He shouldn't be a role model for our students.

For reasons I still do not fully comprehend, my father hired Mercado in spite of my objections. My father was a good-hearted man. He realized that Mercado had studied in our yeshiva and wanted to become part of our faculty. My father was enchanted – shall I say hypnotized – by Mercado's lively personality and glib tongue.

Perhaps my father wanted someone around who could be entertaining. I imagine that he thought Mercado was just one big joke. Certainly, Mercado knew enough to teach the lowest-level classes, but not much more than that. And he has not advanced much since then. He is a man without deep Torah knowledge, without stature in the Torah world. He comes from nowhere, he is nothing, he is going nowhere.

When I become rosh yeshiva, my first act will be to fire Mercado. He doesn't belong in Yeshivas Lita. He is a bad influence on our students. I never wanted him here, and I don't want him here now. To even imagine that Mercado would be appointed rosh yeshiva causes me profound indignation. I tell you, Members of the Search Committee, without equivocation: I would quit this yeshiva if Mercado were appointed rosh yeshiva. Not only would I leave, I know that many of the other faculty members would walk out as well. Yeshivas Lita would fall apart. All the years of effort and energy that have gone into creating this magnificent place of Torah will be dissipated in a matter of weeks. I cannot believe that you would allow this to happen.

I have heard it said by some that I am jealous of Mercado. Jealous! I should be jealous of that lightweight? This gossip is utter nonsense. I know far more Torah than he will ever know. I come from a great line of rabbinic sages. I teach the highest classes in our yeshiva. I am constantly invited to lecture at different yeshivos and synagogues. The public recognizes me, with all due humility, as the leading Torah figure of our generation in the Diaspora. So what basis is there for the canard that I am jealous of Mercado? If anything, he has good reason to be jealous of me!

Ever since he began studying at this yeshiva, I feel he has shown a singular antipathy toward me. I don't know why. I have never tried to hurt him. Whenever I felt I needed to discipline him, I did so for his own good and the good of the yeshiva. It wasn't from malice or vengeance, but from a sense of duty. For two years, he was a student in my class. He was nothing but trouble. He always tried to ask questions that would stump or embarrass me. He stirred up the students against me. He undermined my authority whenever he could. I discussed him at length with Rav Yosef, my father, and my father spent considerable time with him. Regrettably, Rav Yosef liked Mercado and spoiled him. He told me to put up with him patiently. My father felt that Mercado had some special talents and insights. I assured him that this was not so, that Mercado was a troublemaker. But my father, in his infinite kindness, continued to insist on keeping Mercado in our yeshiva – and in my class.

Yes, those were difficult years for me. And yes, I was outraged when Mercado was appointed to our yeshiva's faculty. I feel, though, that I have been able to contain him by keeping him assigned only to the lowest and least desirable classes. I have managed to steer most of the good and promising students into the classes of other members of our faculty. I have kept him as isolated as possible, given the circumstances.

I assure you, Members of the Search Committee, that I have done this for the sake of Heaven, not for my own honor or satisfaction. I feel that he is a dangerous element in our yeshiva.

You may ask: Why is he so dangerous? First, he is not reverent to our yeshiva's classic method of Talmudic study. He creates doubts and dissatisfaction in his students. He negates our authority. Mercado is known to quote from secular sources, from pagan sources, from Christian and Muslim scholars. This is a yeshiva, not a university! Students come here to be instilled with pure Torah knowledge and fear of God. Why does he confuse them with the words of individuals who do not even believe in our Torah? What can such individuals teach our students other than heresy and apostasy? We don't need their ideas, and we don't want their words!

Our Torah tradition has all wisdom within it. We must not dilute or compromise our beloved Torah!

Mercado often speaks in praise of modernity. He has written several articles calling for "modern methods of Torah study." This would be laughable if it were not so tragic. What does he mean by "modern methods," and how can anything "modern" improve upon the age-old and time-tested methods of Torah study sanctified by generations of our sages? He likes to depict me as following "old-fashioned" and "outdated" methods. He thinks this is a criticism, but to me, it is the greatest praise. The Torah is ancient, and the true methods of Torah study are ancient. The fools who prate about modern methods and modern insights do not understand Torah! They are outside of our camp! They chase after false gods!

The great sage, the Chasam Sofer, said it well nearly one hundred and fifty years ago: that which is new is forbidden by the Torah. Innovations are both unnecessary and dangerous. Those who call for changes thereby undermine the authority of our sages; they think they know better than all the Torah giants of our generation and the generations before us. Calls for modernization are simply disguised ways of saying: Let us abandon Torah, let us abandon our traditions, let us find truth elsewhere. Let us adapt to the society around us.

Many Jews have been enticed to modernize. The past several hundred years have witnessed numerous efforts at reform. What has been the result of this approach? Assimilation! Intermarriage! Breakdown in religious observance! Desecration of the Torah! Repudiation of our sages! This, my friends, is where modernization leads. Once the process begins, we find that we are on a slippery slope. Inexorably, we are drawn to chaos and destruction.

21

Yeshivas Lita was established precisely to counteract the tendency towards modernization. My grandfather, Rav Leibel, was a stalwart of traditionalism. He knew that modernity was like a gold ring in a swine's snout. The gold ring glitters. It is attractive. But it is attached to an impure, vile beast. Modernity glitters and is attractive, but it is attached to the beast of godlessness, materialism, immorality. People like Mercado are seduced by the gold ring; they are too blind to see the swine to which the ring is attached.

Members of the Search Committee, you are charged with an enormous and historic responsibility. You are not simply going to decide who will be the rosh yeshiva. You will be deciding the very future of our institution. You will be determining which ideology will infuse our yeshiva in the coming years, and perhaps for generations to come. Are you faithful to our mission? Are you committed to continuing the true pattern set by my grandfather, Rav Leibel, and carried on by my father, Rav Yosef? You know in your hearts that I am the natural heir to their throne, that I alone can carry on in their holy and righteous traditions.

I implore you: do not disgrace yourselves and our yeshiva by turning from our true and tested path. As far as Mercado is concerned, I trust that you will give him no consideration at all. He certainly deserves no attention from this committee.

My presentation is over. I have answered your questions. I trust that you will appoint me rosh yeshiva in a timely manner so that we may get on with the work of the yeshiva – to increase knowledge of Torah, to walk in God's ways, to sustain holiness in the world.

Rav David Mercado

MEMBERS OF THE SEARCH COMMITTEE: I thank you for inviting me to appear before you today. I am honored to be considered for the position of rosh yeshiva of Yeshivat Lita. Whether or not I am ultimately appointed, I will always be grateful to you for having thought me worthy of this interview.

You asked me to explain why I think I am qualified to serve as the rosh yeshiva. I will answer you by describing a bit about my past, how I happened to come to this yeshiva, and the nature of the classes I have been teaching these past years.

I was born and raised in Portland, Oregon. My paternal grandparents had come to Portland in 1908 from the town of Tekirdag, Turkey. My maternal grandparents had come separately as teenagers during the second decade of the century. They had been born and raised on the island of Marmara, about a two-hour boat ride from Istanbul and an hour boat ride to Tekirdag. They were married in Portland in 1922.

Both sets of my grandparents were pious but simple Jews. They had little formal education. My paternal grandfather owned a fruit and vegetable stand; my maternal grandfather was a shoe-maker.

My parents, both of whom were born in Portland, went to public school through high school. Then my mother went to work in a local factory, while my father went into the grocery business. All my uncles and aunts had similar circumstances. They were hard-working, honest, solid citizens. None was rich, or went to college. But they were a happy and good group of people, and I thank the Almighty that I was privileged to grow up among them.

Religion was important to them, but they were not highly trained in Torah studies. My grandfathers could read Hebrew, of course. But their knowledge of Torah and Jewish law came largely from their own parents and grandparents. They also read from the *Me'am Lo'ez*, the classic Biblical compendium which was printed in their vernacular tongue, Ladino – Judeo-Spanish.

I attended the public schools of Portland through high school. I received a little Jewish education at our synagogue's Sunday school; but mostly, I gained knowledge through experience. I learned Judaism by living according to the traditions maintained by my parents and grandparents.

When I graduated high school in 1967, I decided that I would attend Reed College in Oregon. My parents were proud that I was accepted into this prestigious institution, and they threw a special party in my honor. I was the first member of our family to be going to college.

Why did I choose to go to Reed College? Perhaps you in New York do not know about Reed. It was – and still is – an avant-garde place of learning. At Reed, there were no grades, no tests, no papers. Students studied in freedom; they searched for truth as their hearts directed them. Reed was an intellectual's dream – a place to explore all aspects of human knowledge in a serious environment. The faculty members were gifted thinkers. The students were lovers of ideas.

In my senior year of high school, I decided – like many young people – that I wanted to find truth. The more I read, the hungrier I became for knowledge. I was drawn to Reed as metal shavings are drawn to a magnet. I had no idea what I would do once I finished college: what I would do for a living, what I would be fit to do after receiving such an eclectic and impractical education. I knew, though, that I wanted to seek truth, and I put that above practical, mundane considerations.

I spent two wonderful years at Reed. I explored ancient and modern philosophy, astronomy, anthropology, world literature. I took classes in music and poetry, art and physics, Latin and geography. I read voraciously. We students stayed up all hours of the night discussing ideas, debating points of logic, proving and refuting various theorems. The environment was open and inviting. I don't think the academies of Plato or Aristotle could have been more intellectually alive than Reed.

For all my enthusiasm about learning, though, I still felt an emptiness in my soul. Many years later, when I read *The Kuzari* by Rabbi Yehuda Halevy, I realized that I was like the king of the Khazars who heard God's voice in a dream: Your intentions are good but your actions are not. I, too, felt that my intentions were good – but somehow I had a vacuum within myself. Something was not right, something was not complete. I discussed my dilemma with my mother, whose wisdom was a constant source of inspiration to me. She told me: You have begun to seek truth at Reed College. Perhaps it is time that you begin to seek truth in our own Jewish tradition. I thought: My mother is right! The Jewish people has produced numerous sages and philosophers going back thousands of years. Surely our tradition must be incredibly powerful to have survived so long, in so many contexts, under such adverse conditions.

At that time, a rabbi from New York happened to be visiting Portland, looking into the possibility of establishing a new Jewish day school there. I met with him and had a long conversation about my search for truth. He told me that I should consider spending several years studying in the intense Torah atmosphere of a yeshiva. If I would do that, he suggested, I would be well rewarded spiritually and intellectually. "Will I find the answers to my questions?" I asked him. "Probably not," he replied, "but you will find that your questions will have resolved themselves. You may not have your answers, but you will not have your questions either."

The rabbi, who was a graduate of Yeshivat Lita, called Rav Yosef Grossman and told him about me. Rav Yosef was intrigued, but was not quite sure how I could attend Yeshivat Lita. After all, Yeshivat Lita was geared for advanced students, not for beginners. At that time, I could read Hebrew fluently, but without comprehension. My knowledge of Torah was small; my knowledge of Talmud was non-existent. Rav Yosef gave me the following mandate: I should study with a tutor for one year. If I could make adequate progress, he would accept me as a student in Yeshivat Lita in August 1970.

I discussed the matter with my parents, and they agreed that I could leave Reed in order to study Torah with a tutor. My father promised to cover my expenses for two years. After that, he hoped I would undertake to support myself. He was a bit nervous about my impractical, intellectual tendencies, and he wanted to reassure himself – and me – that I would eventually accept the responsibility to make a living on my own. I understood my father's concern and appreciated his legitimate interest in my future.

As there was no satisfactory tutor for me in Portland, I moved to Seattle where I studied with an elderly, retired Sephardic rabbi who had come to Seattle from Istanbul, Rav Ezra Barceloni. With infinite patience and strict discipline, Rav Ezra not only taught me technical skills, he taught me to feel the presence of God when we studied sacred texts.

I will not pretend that I became a fine scholar in that one year, but I did make considerable progress. Rav Ezra was very orderly. We studied Hebrew grammar, Biblical Hebrew, Aramaic. After I had made sufficient progress with the language skills, we then proceeded to study actual texts. First, we studied the Torah itself, spending six hours and more per day analyzing the text, reading the commentaries. Then, we moved to the study of Mishnah, and finally to Gemara. Each day, we also spent two hours studying the code of Jewish law compiled by Maimonides. This study was valuable not merely for an understanding of Jewish law, but also for Hebrew language: Maimonides was a brilliant Hebrew stylist. And perhaps above all, Maimonides was extraordinarily organized. No one before or since has been able to match his achievement.

Although Rav Ezra was an elderly man, he never seemed to tire or run out of energy. Day and night, we studied, we talked, we discussed, we argued. I have never had such a teacher before or since, not in the university and not in the yeshiva.

The year passed and Rav Ezra called Rav Yosef at Yeshivat Lita. He told Rav Yosef what I had accomplished, as well as what I had not been able to accomplish. All in all, Rav Ezra gave me a strong recommendation. Did I know enough to be admitted to Yeshivat Lita? No, I certainly did not know enough. I would be far behind the other students. But, said Rav Ezra, I was a quick learner with an agile mind. I would catch up with the others in a year or two, and would pass most of them in three or four years. Rav Yosef was satisfied. I was admitted.

When I arrived in New York in August 1970, it was the first time I had ever been so far away from my family. Moreover, being a Sephardic Jew, I had no knowledge whatever of Yiddish. My vernacular was English; my parents and grandparents conversed in Judeo-Spanish. Rav Yosef put me in a class of a young teacher who used English as the language of instruction. Rav Yosef told me that some of the more advanced classes were given in Yiddish, and that I had better start learning Yiddish.

At first, I floundered in class. My level of Talmudic knowledge was significantly inferior to that of my classmates – most of whom had been studying Talmud since they were young children. I couldn't follow the lessons for the first few months. I almost reached the point of desperation, thinking I would leave the yeshiva and return to Reed. But my teacher, sensing my frustration, took me aside and assured me that I could and would succeed. He reminded me that the great Rabbi Akiva had not begun to study Torah until he was forty years old, and yet, he went on to become the leading sage of the people of Israel and one of the pillars of Jewish law.

With these words of encouragement, I devoted myself to my studies with even greater zeal. Whatever intellectual ability the Almighty gave me, I applied in full to mastering lines and pages of Talmud. Most of my fellow students were helpful, although a few seemed irritated with my ignorance and were annoyed when I asked elementary questions in class. All in all, I made progress. I felt myself growing stronger and more confident.

At the end of my first year at Yeshivat Lita, I had turned twenty-two years old. My father had told me that he could not support me beyond that point. I had to take responsibility for myself.

I met with Rav Yosef and told him that I had gained much from my year at the yeshiva. I wanted to continue, but I had no financial means to enable me to do so. I needed to find work of some sort. Moreover, I was engaged to be married, and my fiancée was expressing concerns about our future. I needed to focus on a career.

Rav Yosef, who had always displayed a sincere warmth and kindness toward me, said that he had been following my progress closely. He had met regularly with my teacher, who had informed him that I was doing remarkably well and that I should be encouraged to devote my life to Torah study. Rav Yosef told me: You will stay in the yeshiva next year, and the year after, and as long as we can keep you here. You will learn and you will become a real *talmid chochom*. Your wife will work and will support you for the next few years. After that, you will be given employment by our yeshiva – you will become a teacher yourself. You will become one of our rebbeim. This is a good environment for you, and you are good for our yeshiva. So it is settled, yes? I nodded my head yes. It was settled.

The next several years were difficult, but I made steady progress. My wife, a true woman of valor, was happy to work and support me during this period of study. She shared my devotion to Torah and truth, and she looked forward to my reaching the level where I myself could become a rabbi and teacher.

In my fourth year at the yeshiva, I was placed in the class of Rav Shimshon Grossman. Rav Shimshon, unlike his father, seemed to take an immediate dislike to me. He treated me with disdain; he tried to embarrass me by asking questions that he knew I could not answer. The situation grew so unpleasant that I had a meeting with Rav Yosef and requested that he transfer me to another class. He nodded knowingly and told me that I must remain in Rav Shimshon's class. If I could get through two years with Rav Shimshon, he assured me, I will have proven myself a capable student and a promising rabbi.

I tried very hard to concentrate on the lessons, to avoid personal confrontations with Rav Shimshon, to remain silent when he criticized me. All the students thought of Rav Shimshon as a great Talmudist, a brilliant mind. They venerated him – and he knew it, and enjoyed it! But I was not so impressed with him. Indeed, I thought he was an adequate scholar, but not an extraordinary one. But who was I to judge? I was still an ignorant upstart.

One day, Rav Shimshon was discussing a case in Jewish law that had created controversy in the eighteenth century. A woman had brought a chicken to a shochet to be slaughtered. The shochet killed the bird and then examined the innards to see that everything was in proper order. To his surprise, he did not find the chicken's heart. Everything else looked fine, but there was no heart!

One rabbi ruled that the chicken was certainly kosher. It is impossible for a chicken to have lived without a heart. Perhaps the shochet had inadvertently dropped the heart, or perhaps the heart was particularly small and the shochet mistook it for another organ. Whatever the case, since everything else about the chicken looked fine, we may assume its heart was also unblemished.

Another rabbi, though, objected to this ruling. He argued that the chicken was not kosher because it was missing a vital organ – the heart. If the shochet did not find the heart, this means that the chicken had no heart. How, you may ask, can a chicken have lived without a heart? The answer is that the Almighty has the power to create chickens without hearts! This chicken must have had its blood circulated by some other organ. No miracle is beyond God's power.

When Rav Shimshon cited this debate, I must have giggled. I thought it ridiculous to suggest that the chicken had been created without a heart. Obviously, the heart was simply lost or misidentified by the shochet.

Rav Shimshon turned to me in a rage and asked why I was laughing. I explained as calmly as I could that I thought the second rabbi's argument was farfetched. Did God have no other miracles to perform than to create a chicken without a heart? The rest of the class broke out into laughter. Rav Shimshon's face reddened with anger.

He told me that I was a person of little faith, a skeptic, an ignorant nobody. I was guilty of belittling the teachings of a Torah giant, even though I was not worthy of kissing the ground he had walked on.

Upon hearing this attack on me, I rose to my feet – still very calmly – and told Rav Shimshon that he had no right to shame me in public, that it was a terrible sin to humiliate anyone, even an ignoramus such as myself. I told him that if he wanted to believe in chickens without hearts, he was welcome to do so. But he should not expect intelligent people with even a modicum of scientific knowledge to accept such nonsense.

Rav Shimshon ordered me to leave the class. That evening, Rav Yosef called me to his office and told me that I had been wrong to enter into a confrontation with Rav Shimshon. Even if I thought Rav Shimshon was wrong, my duty as a student was to remain silent and respectful. I explained the circumstances to Rav Yosef, and told him why I had felt compelled to respond to Rav Shimshon's unwarranted attack on me. Rav Yosef said: You claim that you came to this yeshiva to search for truth. I am telling you that you cannot search with freedom unless you learn to submit entirely to authority. The kabbalists teach: Wisdom comes from nothingness. Only when you reach the nothingness within yourself will you then be able to build a foundation for truth. Submit. Lower yourself. Learn to accept what you are taught. Then, when your belly is filled with Torah, when you become a true bridegroom of Torah – only then will the truth start to become clear to you. If Rav Shimshon tortures you, consider this to be a test from Heaven. He is a learned and wise rabbi. He is your rebbe and you must see yourself as his faithful disciple.

The next morning, with great anguish in my soul, I entered Rav Shimshon's class and sat in my seat. He smirked at me with self-satisfied, victorious eyes. Then he ignored me completely for the next few months. He did not call on me when I raised my hand. He did not ask me to read the text in class. It was as though I did not exist to him. I kept Rav Yosef's words in mind, and held my peace.

Then another crisis erupted. Rav Shimshon delivered a complex discourse, attempting to resolve a contradiction in the text of Maimonides's code of law. He droned on and on, citing proofs and refutations, arguments and counter-arguments. He drew subtle distinctions, and then even more subtle distinctions. At last, he concluded with his resolution of the difficulty in the text of Maimonides. Abruptly, he turned to me and asked for my opinion of his explanation.

I should have remained silent. I should have nodded my head in approval. But deep within me, I was troubled not only with Rav Shimshon's answer, but by his entire methodology. I could not hold myself back. I responded: Rav Shimshon, the seeming difficulty in the text of Maimonides is no difficulty at all. Your resolution, however ingenious, is entirely unnecessary and untrue. I studied this exact text some years ago with Rav Ezra Barceloni in Seattle. Rav Ezra pointed out the apparent contradiction in the text, but then showed me a commentary on Maimonides by a Yemenite rabbi, a scholar of Maimonides. That rabbi, who had studied various manuscripts of Maimonides's code of Jewish law, especially the Yemenite manuscripts, pointed out that our printed text of Maimonides is incorrect. If we read the Yemenite text of this passage, we see that there is no contradiction at all, and that Maimonides makes perfect sense.

Rav Shimshon exploded. "You skeptic, you phony!" he shouted at me. "What do we care about some manuscript in Yemen? We follow the printed text as we have it. This is the authoritative text and we do not, and may not, veer from it. The fact that our text has been the standard text of Maimonides for the past many centuries means that the Almighty Himself wants us to use this text. We do not need to take into consideration this manuscript or that manuscript. That is the way of modern scholarship, which attempts to undermine our traditions and break the yoke of Torah authority."

I bowed my head and did not respond.

In the weeks and months that followed, I grew increasingly alienated from Rav Shimshon. I felt that his method of study was erroneous. To be sure, he had learned this method from Rav Yosef who had learned it from Rav Leibel who had learned it from the great sages of Lithuania and Poland. This was the method used by all the yeshivot in America, Israel and wherever yeshivot existed. I could excuse the sages of earlier generations for remaining loyal to their traditional methodology. Yet why should modern-day rabbis ignore the fruits of modern scholarship? Why should they be oblivious to the voluminous research on the manuscripts of the Talmud, Maimonides and other classic texts? Why should they teach the pages of Talmud as though they were dropped from heaven in their present form?

My professor of Latin at Reed College had taught us the hazards of transmission of ancient manuscripts and of the copyists' mistakes that naturally and inevitably creep into texts. He taught us how to identify the archetype text, and how to trace a line of errors through manuscripts of succeeding generations. The Talmud and Maimonides's Code of Law are texts with histories of transmission. Minor scribal errors inevitably crept in, and were compounded from generation to generation. So why shouldn't we – students of these texts – know their textual history in manuscript and published form?

I felt that Rav Shimshon's genius was a very narrow genius. He worked entirely within a closed framework, impervious to any ideas, insights, or knowledge that might be available from sources outside his worldview. His lectures were stale and stuffy, the result of working only within a narrow range.

At the conclusion of my first year in Rav Shimshon's class, I met with Rav Yosef and implored him to assign me to another teacher. Again, he refused my request. He explained: If you don't approve of Rav Shimshon's methods, then you are at war with our entire yeshiva system. It is fine to be at war if it is a war for the sake of Heaven. Your insights are fascinating to me and you have much to teach all of us. You won't teach us, however, unless you first understand us fully, and unless you know how to introduce new concepts in a way that does not threaten and undermine our system. It is permissible to innovate, but only after you are thoroughly rooted in our ways. You will be in Rav Shimshon's class for one more year and then we will see what we will do with you.

Rav Yosef, ever mindful of my personal needs, arranged for me to tutor several students so that I might earn some income. My wife and I were expecting our first child. I could not expect my wife to keep working to support me for too much longer.

To make a long story short, my next year in Rav Shimshon's class was not much happier than my first year. He tormented me. His lessons struck me as being dull, plodding, unimaginative. I had come to Yeshivat Lita in search of truth, but now I was stuck with Rav Shimshon!

In spite of my difficulties with Rav Shimshon, I made excellent headway in my studies. I was now recognized as one of the better students. I spent many hours studying Talmud and halakha. I also began to make time for mussar study, Jewish philosophy, and modern Hebrew literature. I even found a little time for secular books.

At the end of the next year, Rav Yosef conferred rabbinical ordination on me and assigned me to teach a class at Yeshivat Lita. Rav Shimshon was livid and would not talk to me. I know that he tried his best to dissuade Rav Yosef from granting me *semikha* and from hiring me to teach in the yeshiva. Rav Yosef, may he rest in peace, resisted his son's entreaties against me.

During the past years, I have been teaching Talmud and I have introduced some new methods – slowly and without fanfare. My students have become aware of the need for textual study. They have learned something of the history of the Talmudic text, and they have learned not to engage in fanciful *pilpul* but to seek truth and clarity. I feel that I must be at least somewhat successful as a teacher, since many of my students request to remain in my class year after year. A number of students choose to be in my class, even though they are eligible to be advanced to Rav Shimshon's class.

Why do I think myself qualified to be the rosh yeshiva of Yeshivat Lita? Because I have worked hard here, because I have learned much here, because I have taught much here, because I have begun to find truth here, because I bring new energy and fresh insights into the studies of our students.

You have asked me, Members of the Search Committee, to comment on my vision for the future of our yeshiva. I will be forthright with you and will not mince words.

I believe our yeshiva attracts the most outstanding students of Torah in America, but I also believe that the yeshiva's system of education is antiquated. I would like this yeshiva to be at the fore-

front of revitalizing and modernizing Torah study. We will empha-
size language and grammar, textual analysis, clear reasoning with
the goal of finding truth. We will not tolerate the convoluted pilpu-
listic style of argumentation. Rather, our guide in language, content
and form will be the works of Maimonides.

I would like to suggest a change in the name of our yeshiva. It
should no longer be called Yeshivat Lita, but Yeshivat America.
The yeshiva's origins were in Lita – yes, that is true. But that is the
past. We need to concentrate on the future, and the future of our
yeshiva is New York – America. We draw students from different
backgrounds – not just Lithuanian and Polish backgrounds. We
need our students to become familiar with the Torah contributions
of a wide variety of sages, not just those who have made it into the
Yeshivat Lita curriculum. After all, Torah scholarship has been
produced by sages who lived all over the world, not just in Eastern
Europe, and by rabbis who spoke various languages, not just Yiddish. Why should our students be deprived of this vast universe of
Torah discourse?

I would like this yeshiva to be a bastion of intellectual freedom.
I want students to think, to ask questions, to search for truth. I
want them to know not only Torah and Talmud, but the wisdom of
the nations as well. I know that my own Torah knowledge has been
powerfully strengthened by my worldly studies. We want our students to be exposed to art and science, to world literature and
music. We want them to recognize that they are not merely Jews.
They are human beings, part of human history and civilization.
They have a responsibility to themselves, to the Jewish people, to
the world at large. They need to have a broad vision of their role in
human society.

It has long distressed me that our students are molded into one image: they all wear black pants, white shirts, black hats. They walk with a certain "yeshiva stoop"; they are pale, they live in a closed, indoors world. Our yeshiva should foster sound minds in sound bodies. We want diversity among our students. Let them not be squeezed into one conformist mode, but let them use their own minds to decide how they will dress and how they will organize their free time. The yeshiva should not be an artificial greenhouse, but an open garden.

Our institution should prepare first-rate scholars who can function successfully in the world. Our students should not be narrow-minded, self-righteous intellectual gymnasts, but should strive to learn from everyone and everything. They should be rabbis and teachers who understand human nature, who can inspire their communities to righteousness.

This, then, is my vision for the future of Yeshivat Lita – or may I say Yeshivat America – an open, intellectually alive, dynamic, creative institution where young men search for truth in an atmosphere of openness and freshness.

I hope, also, that our yeshiva will soon establish a similar institution for young women. Women, after all, also have minds, also need intellectual nurturing, and also play a vital role in society.

Now, I come to your last question: why do I believe I am the most qualified candidate for the office of rosh yeshiva? Members of the Search Committee, I do not know whether I am the most qualified candidate! I do not claim to be the most learned or the most famous or the most popular. If you want the yeshiva to continue on its present course, then I am surely not the best candidate – Rav Shimshon is!

I hope, though, that you will see that this is a turning point in the history of our yeshiva. We have an opportunity to build on our strengths and redirect our energies, to move the yeshiva in a new path. We can shake off cobwebs of the past while retaining the essential strengths of the past. We must focus, though, on creating a future that is not merely a clone of the past. We and our students live now, not in the past. We live in America, not in Lita. We must draw on the fruits of modern research and scholarship, not be locked into a closed box.

If you share these feelings, Members of the Search Committee, then perhaps you will judge me to be the best candidate – if for no other reason than because I am the only candidate available who advocates these ideas.

I thank you for your kind consideration and for your attention. May the Almighty bless your deliberations.

Mrs. Deena Leah Grossman

MEMBERS OF THE SEARCH COMMITTEE: I appear before you as
you have requested. I must tell the truth: I think it is quite irregular
and unnecessary for you to have summoned me. It is my husband
who is to be selected as rosh yeshiva. Surely I can have little or no
impact on this matter. I am merely his wife, and I am not a
candidate for any other position!

You have asked me to respond to three questions, and I will do
so. I respond not because I think it is necessary or appropriate, but
only to avoid the appearance of being uncooperative. My husband
agreed that I should answer your questions, although he, too, objects to your impertinence in summoning me.

Here are the questions you have asked me. Number one: do I
want my husband to be the rosh yeshiva? Number two: what role
should the wife of the rosh yeshiva play in the yeshiva? Number
three: what do I think of our system of *shidduchim* for our students?

Number one: of course I want my husband to be rosh yeshiva! What can you have had in mind when you formulated this question? My husband is the greatest Torah luminary in America and I have always had the fullest confidence and expectation that he would become the rosh yeshiva of Yeshivas Lita. Among our circle of friends, it has always been an unstated assumption that my husband would one day become the rosh yeshiva. So, of course, I want – and expect – my husband to be appointed to this position.

In a sense, this yeshiva is a family business. It was established by my husband's grandfather, and was led for many years by my father-in-law, of blessed memory. Rav Yosef had no doubt that his son would take over the helm of the yeshiva. It is only a pity that he did not make a public announcement appointing his son as his successor. But everyone knows that this is what he had in mind to do.

As you probably know, I am the daughter of Rabbi Berel Shoichet, who was himself a great *talmid chochom*. My father was very keen on arranging my marriage to Rav Yosef's son specifically because he believed that Rav Yosef's son would become the rosh yeshiva of Yeshivas Lita one day. My father told me: My dear Deena Leah, you cannot be a rosh yeshiva because you are only a woman, but at least I can have a son-in-law who will wear the crown of the kingdom of a large yeshiva. I was proud to be able to be part of my father's ambition and dream.

I have been a devoted wife and mother. I have helped my husband in every way possible. I have rejoiced in his accomplishments; I have encouraged him when he has faced disappointment and frustration. I have always told him: Don't be bothered by petty people and petty events. You are destined to be rosh yeshiva and to be recognized as the greatest Torah scholar of our generation. You will raise a new generation of rabbis and teachers just as your father and grandfather before you led their generations.

Some people think that I am haughty. I am not haughty. I – through my father and through my husband – represent the aristocracy of the Torah world. I carry myself with pride not for my own glory, but out of respect for the dignity of the Torah. I insist that my husband carry himself with pride; he is the descendant of noble ancestors, the bearer of tremendous knowledge, the greatest Torah scholar of this generation in America.

Of course I want my husband to be rosh yeshiva. This will be the fulfillment of many years of our dreams. This office is coming to him, and he has earned it.

This brings me to your second question: how do I see the role of the wife of the rosh yeshiva? Let me answer your question with another question. How do you see the role of the First Lady, the wife of the President of the United States? She is not elected to any office. She should not have any responsibilities or privileges. We all know, however, that the First Lady can play an important role in government. Sometimes she has more influence than high officials and advisors. Sometimes she has more power than the President himself!

The wife of the rosh yeshiva is the First Lady of Yeshivas Lita. She plays an important role. First, she must serve the needs of the rosh yeshiva; she must help him, support him, encourage him, guide him. She must also be the female role model for the yeshiva community. Look at me! You see that I am a dignified lady, a woman deeply devoted to our traditions. The younger women look to me as a role model. When my husband is rosh yeshiva, my influence on them will only increase.

I have heard the ludicrous rumor that your committee is giving consideration to the candidacy of Mercado. I assume that this rumor is false. It is so preposterous that it defies all sense of justice and good sense. I shall not speak of Mercado. I do feel obliged, though, to say a few words about his wife. I must tell the truth! I am not cowardly like so many others who keep silent in the face of outrageous behavior.

If Mercado is unfit to be rosh yeshiva, his wife is even less fit to be the rosh yeshiva's wife. She acts and dresses in ways that are not only inappropriate, but that violate Jewish law and custom. She is a disgrace to our yeshiva now – all the more so if she were, Heaven forbid, to be the wife of the rosh yeshiva.

Look at me! You see that I cover my hair as is proper according to the halakha. I not only wear a wig in public, but I also wear a hat on top of my wig. In contrast, Mercado's wife appears in public without a hair covering – not a wig, not a hat, not a kerchief – nothing at all! And look at the way I dress – modestly, in sedately-colored clothing. I do not say that Mercado's wife dresses immodestly exactly – but her manner of dress reflects her poor values. Her clothing is often colorful, even flamboyant. She calls attention to herself.

Nor is this all! She speaks openly and as an equal in the company of men. She does not maintain the high standard of modesty and gentleness that have always characterized women of the Torah community. She is brazen. She looks right into the eyes of men when she speaks to them. She argues with them and contradicts them, as though she had a perfect right to do so. But this is intolerable! Good women, God-fearing women, practice the virtue of

MARC ANGEL

modesty, silence, deference to Torah scholars. Not Mercado's wife! She thinks she may say what she wishes when she wishes!

One of her basic problems is that she attended college. She lived in the world of hedonism and heresy typical of American colleges. She absorbed foreign values and ideas. She got "liberated." Once exposed to the impurity of college, very few people can regain purity and holiness. Their souls have been defiled and corrupted. I am afraid that Mercado's wife is a lost cause when it comes to true fear of Heaven and love of God. She has been contaminated.

She writes poetry! She writes short stories! I hear she is now working on a novel! If her literary work were for the sake of bringing people closer to Torah, perhaps it could be justified. I, of course, have never read a word of her writings. I don't have time to waste on such drivel. But when other women approached me to tell me about Mercado's wife's literary efforts, they asked me to use my influence to get her to stop.

I took her aside one day – a number of years ago – and told her that the women of our yeshiva community were not pleased with her literary activities. I told her: I must tell the truth! You should be devoting yourself to Torah and good deeds, not to writing for publication. It is neither appropriate nor modest for you to engage in such secular activity.

What do you think her response was? What do you think she told me, wife of Rav Shimshon, daughter of Rav Berel, and daughter-in-law of Rav Yosef? She told me to mind my own business!

I reminded her that everything having to do with the reputation of our yeshiva was my business! It is – and always will be – my business to help maintain the high religious standards of our community. We must not allow ourselves to become the laughingstock of the yeshiva world.

She replied: I write because I love words, images, beauty. I have the need to express my feelings and ideas. Literature is the voice of humanity. I, too, have a voice. I want to share my voice with humanity.

Members of the Search Committee, I ask you: Is this the response you would expect from a genuinely religious woman, from the wife of a rabbi who teaches classes in Yeshivas Lita? Surely this is intolerable! It is an outrage!

She is an outsider. I have heard plenty of things about her background, but I naturally keep these things to myself. I am not a gossip or slanderer. But I can assure you – knowing what I know – that she doesn't belong here and has never belonged here. It is a source of pain to me that my father-in-law, Rav Yosef, of blessed memory, was so tolerant with Mercado and his wife. He let things pass that should have been strictly forbidden. He spoiled them, not realizing how bad an influence they are on our community. I am sure you realize that I tried – and Rav Shimshon tried – to persuade Rav Yosef to send Mercado and his wife away from our yeshiva. Regrettably, we failed to convince him. What a pity!

Let me go to your third question: what do I think about our system of arranging marriages? I must tell the truth: I fail to understand the intent of your question. It seems to imply that there may be something wrong with our system, or that people are suggesting changes in our system.

The fact is: our system is time-tested and time-proven. The young men who study in our yeshiva all need to get married. On this, everyone agrees. They are so immersed in their Torah study

that they do not have much spare time to engage in long court-
ships. Moreover, since they are ignorant in the ways of the world,
how could they possibly be trusted to choose proper wives for
themselves? They are young and inexperienced. The choice of a
suitable wife is beyond their abilities.

So we have our system of *shidduchim*. Fathers with eligible
daughters come to the yeshiva in search of proper sons-in-law. Our
committee – I have chaired this committee for many years now –
decides who would be appropriate for whom. We take into consideration matters of *yichus*, *midos*, and also matters of *gashmiyus*. Many
of our boys come from homes of modest financial means. They
wish to study Torah in our yeshiva as long as they possibly can,
years and years. When they finally finish their studies at Yeshivas
Lita, most will become teachers and rabbis and will earn small sala-
ries. So how are they to support themselves and their families if
they are dedicating their lives to Torah? The answer often is that
they need to find wives who come from wealthy families who will
support them. Or they need wives who are willing to work to earn
the income necessary to support their husbands. What greater virtue can there be for a woman than to support her husband, who is
dedicating his life to Torah study? This is an ideal of the highest
magnitude.

So our committee chooses a suitable wife for each of our students. They go out on several dates. If they seem to get along, they
become engaged. The families then work out details, the wedding is
scheduled, and a new household will be established. I can tell you
that we have done very well over the years. I can also tell you that
the marriages we arrange are far happier and more stable than marriages in the outside world. When you leave it to young men and

women to make their own choices, they often make the wrong choices. They don't know what's really important in a partner. They usually make their decisions based only on physical attraction and external beauty – the hedonism and materialism that characterize outside society. Their marriages don't last. The divorce rate in the outside world is skyrocketing.

In all the years I have been involved in this mitzvah, I can tell you this: we have never – I say never – considered any young lady who has attended an American college. We do not want such women as wives for our yeshiva boys. They are tainted. No, we only consider girls who have been brought up in religious families, who have been educated in all-girl religious schools, and who desire nothing else than to spend their lives devoted to their husbands and children. This is a system that is successful. This is a system that maintains purity and holiness. This is a system where people are really happy because they know they are living their lives for the sake of Heaven.

From time to time, I have heard some objections to our system. Indeed, I believe Mercado's wife is an opponent of our system. I'm not surprised! Since she is a college graduate, we would never even allow her to marry one of our students. So she feels insulted or angered or relegated to the periphery of the yeshiva's inner circle.

The critics complain that our system deprives our young people of freedom. Freedom! Where in the Torah does it say that young people have a right to freedom? They are supposed to get married, have children, and live a life faithful to our traditions. What does freedom have to do with this? If you look at those young people outside our system, those who claim to have freedom, do you find happy, pure, good people? No! You find promiscuity, unfaithfulness, divorce, chaos! Is this kind of freedom something we want for our own beloved young people, our Torah scholars? Of course not! Heaven forbid!

The critics complain that our system exploits women and their families. The women and their families become responsible for supporting the men who study Torah. Is this exploitation? Is supporting Torah scholarship exploitation? What utter nonsense! We are a community, not just a group of stray individuals. We have a purpose, a mission. We want to maintain Torah and transmit Torah to the future generations. To insure this continuity, everyone – man and woman – must play his or her role. The men study and teach Torah. The women support the men and raise the children. This is not exploitation. This is cooperation! This is a joint effort toward building a religious future.

Our yeshiva, along with other yeshivas that share our commitments, does not bow to the immoral fashions of American society. We do not buy into their concepts – freedom of choice, women's liberation, reform, the rights of individuals. These terms are only excuses for people to submit to their animal instincts. Modernity creates phrases and catchwords that sound noble and idealistic, but they are really only intent on one thing: justifying immoral behavior.

In our community, the key phrases are very different: fear of Heaven, submission to religious authority, traditionalism, commitment to the welfare of our people. We do not see ourselves primarily as distinct and distinctive individuals. We see ourselves as part of the eternal Congregation of Israel. Our lives – body and soul – are dedicated with perfect devotion to the continuity of our traditions from generation to generation.

I have answered your questions. I have spent more time here than I had anticipated. I have so many things to do!

I leave you with this message: please complete your deliberations speedily. Please announce the appointment of my husband as rosh yeshiva without further delay. Our yeshiva community needs my husband as rosh yeshiva.

Good day.

Mrs. Sultana Mercado

GOOD EVENING, MEMBERS OF THE SEARCH COMMITTEE. It was kind of you to include me in your series of interviews. I appreciate your thoughtfulness.

I will answer the questions you have posed to me, but I think it would be a good idea first to tell you something about myself. I want to put certain personal facts on the table so that they do not become an issue later.

First, let me tell you that I was not born Jewish. I converted to Judaism in 1972, shortly before I married my husband. I believe there have been some whisperings and gossip about my past, so I want to set the record straight. You may then factor in this information when you reach the point when you have to make a decision about the new rosh yeshiva.

My name is Sultana. Early in this century, that was a popular woman's name among Turks. Jews also used this name. As a rule,

Greeks did not give their daughters this name. Yet I am of Greek background, and my name is Sultana. How did this come about?

My father was born on the island of Marmara. He was the son of a Greek Orthodox fisherman. Before 1920, the town of Marmara had a population of about eight thousand souls – the vast majority being Greeks. There were about three hundred Turks and two hundred Jews.

As a young man, my father fell madly in love with a Jewish young lady whose name was Sultana. The two of them – only teenagers at the time – made an oath that they would one day be married to each other. They were so young, so drawn to each other, so optimistic about the future. But they were also unrealistic.

In those days, it was unheard of for a Greek Christian to marry a Jew. Intermarriage was forbidden by both groups. In fact, the attitudes separating the groups were so intense that it was almost impossible for their young people to contemplate marriage to each other. This was out of bounds entirely. Yet there was my father, Mikael Stavroulakis, and Sultana – and they made a covenant of marriage between themselves. There is an old Greek adage: something is impossible until it becomes possible. And so, the impossible became possible. A Greek man and a Jewish woman fell in love.

When my father informed his father about Sultana, my grandfather immediately cursed him. This could never be. It would be an eternal blot on the family. It was against the will of God and man. My father explained his feelings as best he could, but my grandfather was not open to discussion. There was to be no marriage with a Jew under any circumstances. If Mikael were to disobey his father, he would be disowned and treated like an outcast.

When Sultana informed her father about Mikael, her father was indignant. He told her that her promise to Mikael was sacrilege, that it meant nothing at all; she had no right to make any commitments without her father's permission. There was to be no marriage between Sultana and a Greek, her father warned.

In spite of this wall of opposition, Mikael and Sultana found ways of meeting secretly. They had a special spot at the bottom of a hill outside of town. Atop the hill was a large, unfinished marble structure that the Jews called Casa del Pasha, the Pasha's palace. According to the popular belief, there was once a pasha – a rich and powerful Turkish nobleman – who wanted to impress the world with his wealth and success. He came to the island of Marmara and decided to build a magnificent palace at the top of a great hill overlooking the town, with an unobstructed view of the sea. This palace was to be his summer quarters. He chose Marmara for its beauty as well as for the famous marble deposits on the island.

The project began, and the townspeople watched with wonder as the great marble columns were put in place. This building was, indeed, going to be the most spectacular structure on the island.

But suddenly, all work stopped on the Casa del Pasha. The unfinished structure sitting atop a prominent hill now became something of an eyesore. The rumor spread that the Pasha had fallen out of favor with the Sultan and that he had lost his wealth. He was unable to finish his summer palace and had to abandon the project. The Casa del Pasha became a symbol of the folly of vanity and arrogance. It was a visible reminder of the unpredictable vicissitudes of life. Today one is powerful and wealthy; tomorrow he is ruined. Even the grandest of human plans may go astray.

Mikael and Sultana met near the Casa del Pasha and wondered if their own grand plans would similarly remain unfulfilled. They contemplated eloping, running away to America. But neither of them had any money, and neither wanted to break their parents' hearts. Weeks and months passed, but they could think of no way out of their dilemma.

Meanwhile, Sultana's father saw how deeply his daughter was attached to Mikael. He decided that the only way to salvage the situation was to send Sultana to the United States. That way, she would be so far away from Mikael that a marriage between them would be impossible. With the passage of time, Sultana would come to forget her Greek suitor and would marry a good Jewish man, as was proper. Sultana was informed by her father that she would be leaving Marmara and traveling to Portland, Oregon, where some relatives had already settled. She would live with an uncle and aunt, who promised to look after her until she married. Sultana's opinion and her feelings were not considered. Her father had decided what was best for her, and she was expected to obey his instructions. Although she showed respect and deference to her father, her heart was pounding hard and her blood was boiling.

Sultana fled from her father's presence and found Mikael. They went to the Casa del Pasha and discussed their future. They cried. They pledged eternal love. They promised that they would somehow find a way of reuniting. But in their hearts, they knew that this was to be their last meeting. The Casa del Pasha was a dream that failed, and their hope for marriage was also to become a failed dream. They embraced. They parted.

Within a few days, Sultana was traveling to Naples, Italy, where she would catch her ship to New York. It was 1919, and she was just eighteen years old. She crossed the ocean to America, and then crossed America by train to get to Portland. Her new life had begun.

Mikael was heartbroken. Sultana had promised to write to him from Portland, and she did so upon her arrival there. They corresponded by mail for about six months, and then the letters from Sultana became fewer and fewer. After several months had passed with no letters from Sultana, Mikael received a short note from her telling him that she had married a young Jewish man in Portland. She told Mikael that she would always love him, but that she had to go on with her life. She had found a wonderful husband, and she wanted Mikael to find a wonderful wife. Since marriage between Sultana and Mikael was impossible, they both needed to make new lives for themselves. She wished him the best of luck.

Mikael, though, was so deeply in love with Sultana that he could not imagine himself marrying anyone else. In spite of persistent efforts by his father to arrange a marriage for him with a local Greek young lady, Mikael remained a bachelor. He would never marry, he said. His true love was only Sultana. If he had lost her, he had lost everything.

Life was changing on the island of Marmara. The economy of Marmara – never too good – was deteriorating steadily. Jews were migrating away at a steady pace. Most of the young Jewish men and women went to America. Many of the elder Jews moved to Istanbul. Tensions between the Greeks and Turks of the island grew more hostile than ever. Then, in 1920, an agreement was reached by the governments of Turkey and Greece calling for a population transfer. Greeks living in Turkish domains would be relocated in Greek territory, while Turks living in Greek domains would be relocated in Turkish territory. No one, of course, consulted the people who were to be uprooted.

When word reached the island of Marmara that all Greeks had to pack their things and prepare to move out, the Greeks were confused and angered. They had been living on this island for centuries. They were rooted here, happy here. Why should they be forced to leave their homes, their churches, their cemeteries?

For all their laments and protests, they were given no choice in the matter. They were gathered into ships, carrying whatever possessions they could manage, and were sent to various towns controlled by Greece. They tried to stay together as much as possible, so they would be able to help each other in their new locations. They were demoralized. Some began thinking of settling in America. America was a free and prosperous country. It did not force its people to move from one place to another. It offered opportunity for those who were willing to work hard.

In 1921, though, the American Congress had passed a law limiting immigration. This law sharply reduced the number of immigrants from Greece, among other countries. The Greeks who had been transplanted from Marmara found themselves in a bind. Most of them simply reconciled themselves to their new towns. Some, however, did receive permission for entry into the United States. Among those who received immigration papers was Mikael. In the winter of 1921, he was on a ship headed for New York.

Once he arrived in the United States, Mikael took a train to Tacoma, Washington, where a community of Greeks from Marmara had established a community in the preceding decades. He had some friends and relatives among them. He found work in a paper mill and was eventually promoted to foreman. A number of Greek families with daughters of marriageable age approached Mikael as a prospective husband. He fended them off. He told them that he was a bachelor and would remain so.

Although Tacoma is only several hundred miles away from Portland, Mikael was firm in his decision not to try to find Sultana. It would not be fair to her. Their meeting at this juncture in life would only cause pain and remorse. Nothing good could come of it.

Many years passed. In 1950, when Mikael was nearly fifty years old, his loneliness overcame him. He had martyred himself for Sultana's sake for so long, but now, he finally concluded, he wanted to find a wife. He did not want to spend his old age without a partner.

He proposed marriage to a young Greek widow – about thirty years old at the time – and she accepted. He made only one stipulation. If the Lord blessed them with a daughter, the daughter was to be named Sultana. The widow agreed. In 1952, a daughter was born to them, and sure enough, she was named Sultana. I am their daughter. As things turned out, I was their only child.

I grew up in Tacoma. Although I was active in the Greek-American community there, I was part of the American melting pot. Since I attended public schools from elementary through high school, I had friends and classmates of many different backgrounds. Although being Greek was important to me, I was a born American and I thought of myself as being an organic part of American society.

In the summer of 1970, after I had graduated high school and was preparing to attend Barnard College in New York, the Greek community of Tacoma sponsored a picnic at Point Defiance Park to commemorate the fiftieth anniversary of the transfer of Greeks from Marmara. Publicity went out to the Greek communities in Tacoma, Seattle, and Portland. The picnic's organizers wanted to attract the old-timers who had actually been born and raised in Marmara. This was to be an occasion for nostalgia, a time to reminisce about the old days, and to build a sense of solidarity among the American-born generations.

The Jewish communities of Seattle and Portland, which included a significant group of Jews of Marmarali background, learned of the picnic and they, too, wanted to be included. The day of the picnic arrived, the weather was perfect, and a crowd of several hundred people showed up. It was a great day, a great success.

My parents brought me to the picnic and were proudly showing me off to anyone who would listen. I was their daughter, a proud Greek, and I had been accepted as a student at the elite Barnard College in New York City. As we mingled among the picnickers, I noticed that my father's face suddenly froze, as though he had seen a ghost. In a sense, he had seen a ghost, a ghost of his own past. Sitting at a picnic table not far from us was an elderly woman, beautiful yet, smiling with the radiance of the sun. It was Sultana, the love of his life, the woman after whom I was named!

My father walked slowly toward Sultana, wondering if she would even recognize him after all these years. As he approached, Sultana's eyes turned in his direction and her face, too, filled with an expression of disbelief. "Mikael," she called out quietly. "Yes, Sultana," he responded as he came next to her. They stared into each other's eyes briefly, but a whole book could be written about the meeting of their eyes.

In a moment, my father called out to me and waved for me to come to him. When I drew near, he turned to the elder Sultana.

"Here," he announced proudly, "is my daughter. Her name is Sultana." Then, turning to me, he said: "Sultana, this grand woman was a dear friend of mine when we were youngsters growing up on the island of Marmara. I named you after her. She is the reason you are a Greek woman with the name of Sultana."

Our family spent the rest of the day with Sultana's family. The old story of their love, so long a secret to everyone, was now made public. It was late in both of their lives now, and there seemed to be no more reason to hide their youthful romance. Many years had passed. Sultana was now a grandmother with grown grandchildren. My father, though he married late in life, had a grown, college-bound daughter.

As the members of the two families met, I was immediately attracted to a grandson of Sultana. His name was David Mercado. He was only a year or two older than I, and we naturally fell to talking with each other. I was heading to Barnard College in New York City, and he was heading to Yeshivat Lita in New York City. Both of us were leaving our homes on the west coast to advance our educations in the east – and in the same city, at that.

I don't know how to explain it in words, but David and I immediately had an amazing rapport. It was as though we had always known each other, as though we had been friends since childhood. Perhaps, in some mysterious way, we were a replay of Sultana and Mikael in Marmara. We both felt that our meeting at the picnic was more than blind chance. It was destiny.

When evening came and the festivities ended, the picnickers began to pack their things and head back to their cars. I did not want the moment to end, nor did David. Something had happened to us that day, something that would forever transform our lives.

Somehow we sensed that our lives were bound together, or that they ought to be bound together.

That September, I traveled to New York to begin my studies at Barnard College. No sooner had I been assigned a dorm room and a telephone number than I received a call from David Mercado, who had also just recently arrived in New York. We arranged to meet for a cup of coffee. That meeting lasted several hours. I learned that he had come to Yeshivat Lita to find "truth," to study Torah as deeply as he possibly could. The more he spoke, the more I sensed his unusual idealism and enthusiasm. I told him about my plans to study literature, to become a writer, and possibly a college professor.

We met regularly and our friendship – though neither of us would dare admit it – had deepened into love. He was conflicted about his feelings for me, of that I am certain. He was devoting himself to Torah study. It was absolutely forbidden by his religious teachings for him to marry a non-Jewish woman, yet his heart was increasingly tied to a Greek Christian woman who had the same name as his own grandmother.

I, too, had problems to confront. Yes, I loved David, I respected his integrity, his incredible genius, his inner fire. But I was raised as a Greek Orthodox Christian. I had given up believing many of the teachings of my father's faith when I was still in high school. I hardly observed any of the religious traditions. Yet I still felt bound to the faith and to the community, since I was bound to my father. I would never betray my father's love and trust. Just as David's religion forbade marriage to a non-Jew, so my religion forbade marriage to a Jew. It seemed as though David and I were confronting our own Casa del Pasha, our own dream that could not be fulfilled.

By the spring term, we were seeing each other much less frequently. For one thing, David was so engrossed in his studies he had little time for outside interests. Moreover, this may have been his way of trying to sever the ties between us. He knew that the relationship, as things stood, could have no happy future. I, too, was feeling that we needed to create more distance between us. Otherwise, our ultimate disappointment would be too terrible.

I went to Tacoma for Easter break, and was glad to see my parents after so many months of separation. During that vacation, I had a long private talk with my father. I explained to him how David and I felt about each other, how we were now trying to create separation between ourselves. I told him how strange it was that our situation seemed so similar to the experience of him and Sultana so long ago on the island of Marmara.

My father's eyes filled with tears. "Sultana," he said solemnly, "if you love David and David loves you, then you both must find a way to marry. You must not follow in your father's footsteps in this matter."

"But even if I wanted to marry David, he would not marry me. He cannot marry someone who is not of his faith. David is becoming a scholar, a rabbi. He would not break his traditions."

"Then you must study Judaism and become a Jewess." My father said this calmly and seriously. I was astonished.

"I should become Jewish?" I asked, to be sure I had heard my father correctly.

"Yes, you should. You must become Jewish."

The conversation ended. Easter recess ended. I returned to New York.

It had never occurred to me to become Jewish. I knew next to nothing about Judaism, and that which I learned in church and Sunday school as a child was filled with age-old antisemitic stereotypes.

My father's words, though, had a tremendous, deep impact on me. Perhaps they were exactly the words I wanted and needed to hear.

I made an appointment with the rabbi who served the Jewish students of Barnard and Columbia. I discussed my interest in studying Judaism with the goal of conversion. He was a young Orthodox rabbi. He asked me a few questions, told me of the many difficulties faced by Jews, informed me that God loves all good people, not only good Jews. I need not undergo conversion to be beloved by God. I assured him that I was prepared to begin the road toward conversion. As I learned more about Judaism, I would be in a better position to know whether or not to complete the process. He accepted me as a student.

Once I had actually begun to study Judaism, I wrote David a short note and told him that we should not see each other again. I did not want to hurt him, but I wanted to separate myself from him as much as possible for the time being. I did not tell him I was studying Judaism. I did not want to raise his hopes, nor make my conversion contingent on my relationship with him.

When the college term ended, I chose to remain in New York for the summer in order to take classes in Hebrew and Jewish law — classes that were not available in Tacoma. I also must have been reluctant to return to my parents' home at this early stage in my Jewish studies.

The following spring, just before Passover, my rabbi and teacher stated that he felt I was ready to enter the fold of Israel. I had studied diligently, I had become observant of kashruth, Sabbath, holidays. I had come to feel Jewish, that my destiny was tied to that of the Jewish people. "Your people shall be my people, your God my God." I was ready to follow in the footsteps of Ruth.

The rabbi convened a Beit Din and we met at the mikveh for the formal conversion process. The rabbis asked me questions to assure themselves that I was accepting the beliefs, laws and traditions of the Jewish people of my own free will, with clear awareness of the seriousness of my decision. When all were satisfied that I was ready, I went into the dressing room, entered the mikveh and immersed, as the rabbis stood outside the door. I recited the blessing on the immersion, as well as the blessing thanking God for having sustained me in life so that I could reach this special moment. The mikveh lady then asked me to immerse again, and I did so. I heard the rabbis call out *mazal tov* – congratulations. I was now Jewish. The rabbis asked me what Hebrew name I had chosen for myself. I told them: My name is Sultana. Yes, they said, but you should have a Hebrew name as well. I told them that among Turkish Jews, the name Sultana was a Jewish name. They shrugged their shoulders and finally agreed that my Jewish name would be Sultana.

That afternoon, I called Yeshivat Lita and asked to speak with David Mercado. It had been nearly a year since we last had spoken to each other. After a few minutes of waiting, I heard David's voice on the telephone. "David," I said excitedly, "I need to see you as soon as possible. It is urgent." David seemed confused and surprised, but yes, he said, I'll see you tonight at seven at Famous Dairy Restaurant.

When we met, it was as though there had never been an interruption in our friendship. We were as natural and easy with each other as though we had seen each other yesterday. When we sat down, I pulled out my conversion certificate and passed it to David. "David," I said teasingly, "I have found this Hebrew document. Will you please tell me what it says?"

David read it slowly and carefully, showing no sign of emotion. "Where did you get this?" he asked quietly.

"It was given to me this morning by three rabbis, at the mikveh."

"Are you joking with me?"

"No. I have never been more serious in my life."

"You have converted to Judaism according to halakha?"

"That's what that paper says!"

His face opened with a slow, broad grin. "So you're Jewish? How did this all come about?"

We spent the next several hours talking over the process of my conversion, starting from my conversation with my father. When David was satisfied that everything had been done in complete conformity with halakha, he told me how pleased he was. And then he proposed marriage and I accepted. We set a wedding date for that June and we decided we would be married in Portland, where most of his family resided.

After our wedding, we traveled to Turkey and went to the island of Marmara. We found our way to the hill where the Casa del Pasha still stood, where my father and David's grandmother had said goodbye to each other more than fifty years earlier.

I have given you this account because I think it will help you to understand us better, to have a clearer idea of who we are. If David is to become the rosh yeshiva, his past and my past will be open books. I want you to have the true story, so that you will not be misled by gossip and rumors.

Now, let me answer the questions you have put to me. Do I think my husband should be appointed rosh yeshiva? The answer is yes, without equivocation. He is a gifted and sensitive Torah scholar, wise beyond his years. He is young, enthusiastic, energetic and idealistic, and he is a very effective teacher and leader. He will breathe new life into the yeshiva and help it grow and flourish.

You ask: What do I think should be the role of the wife of the rosh yeshiva? The wife of the rosh yeshiva should be a good wife to her husband – no more, no less. I will support him in all his endeavors, but I will continue my own interests as well. As you may know, I enjoy writing, and have published some poetry and short fiction. I hope to continue with my literary career. David, of course, supports and encourages my writing. Being the wife of the rosh yeshiva does not require – it seems to me – that I abandon my own personal goals and pursuits.

I imagine that some people will not like to see me as wife of the rosh yeshiva. I am too "modern" for them. I don't cover my hair, I wear stylish clothing, I carry myself with pride and confidence. I don't believe that religious women have to look like sacks of potatoes. I think it is foolish and hypocritical for them to wear wigs that often look better than their own hair. I think it is a pity that they feel compelled to wear dumpy hats and snoods, and that they think this is somehow a fulfillment of the religious requirements for modesty. It is not modesty, as much as plain bad taste in fashion.

They are taught that they should cover their hair and dress modestly so that they will not attract the attention of men other than their husbands. Yet their husbands see a great many women whose hair is uncovered and whose clothing is lovely. So the wives may become less attractive in the eyes of their own husbands!

I know that a number of religious women in Europe stopped covering their hair already a century and more ago. Even in such traditional lands as Morocco, the wives of the rabbis and religious functionaries gave up the fashion of hair covering long ago. In the United States, many wives of Orthodox rabbis did not cover their hair during the past several generations. It seems to me – and to my husband – that hair covering for married women today has become something of an identity badge. It is not done so much for religious purposes as to show group solidarity with other Orthodox Jewish women. Just as men have distinctive headwear, women want it too. It gives them a sense of belonging to an in-group.

If my husband is selected as rosh yeshiva, my role will be more as a symbol than as an active participant in his work. Some will criticize my modern ways, and many will engage in gossip against me. (They already do!) But many others will see that there is another alternative for religious women – an alternative that embraces modernity and social progress while remaining deeply faithful to tradition.

This leads me to your third question: the system of *shidduchim* – arranging marriages. The system that has developed in recent years is highly prejudiced against women. Girls are taught from their early years that their goal in life must be to marry a man who studies Torah all day. What does this imply? First, that their own spiritual lives are secondary to those of their husbands. They must make all the sacrifices. Second, it means that they must bear and raise their children, clean the house, cook, and they must also work so that they can earn money to support the family while the husband sits in the yeshiva studying Torah, and does not even teach. Almost the entire burden of the family's material well-being falls on the woman. Third, this system puts a terrible financial strain on the parents of daughters. They have to pay for weddings, they have to help support their daughters' husbands, and often they have to provide financial assistance to their children's families for many years.

Although this system is well-intentioned, it fosters a certain type of corruption of values. It encourages young men to want wives who come from rich families. Daughters from poor families, regardless of their virtues, are less sought-after. The religious community is often critical of what is called American materialism, yet look how deeply materialism has infected our own community! And this materialism is encouraged by the yeshiva establishment, who want wealthy patrons for their students.

The system is not merely exploitative of women and their families, but it is also damaging to the men involved. Students in the yeshiva come to think that their studying Torah is such a lofty enterprise, that they do not have to take responsibility for their lives and the lives of their families. They may develop an attitude that everything is coming to them, that everyone is responsible for maintaining them. As long as they study Torah, they are exempt from worldly concerns. This system fosters a sense of self-righteousness on the part of the young men.

This strategy is psychologically unhealthy and morally repugnant. The yeshiva world is creating a cadre of parasites, men who live off the work of others. The Psalmist has taught that the one who eats from the labor of his own hand is the one who is truly happy. Yet we raise men who do not know what it means to eat from the labor of their own hands, who have come to believe that living off charity is dignified. The more isolated they are from real work and the everyday conflicts of life, the less they can really understand Torah. They confine themselves to a narrow world. They have narrow intellectual horizons. They come to feel disdain for those who do not study Torah full-time.

I know that our yeshiva alone cannot revolutionize the prevalent system of *shidduchim* in the yeshiva world. But we can make some important strides in the right direction. Graduate students in universities may receive grants and stipends to enable them to complete their studies, but then they go out and find jobs. Likewise, our yeshiva should support students for a number of years with the expectation that they will then go out and find jobs. They should be imbued with the self-respect that goes with accepting responsibility for playing a role in society – they will support their families, they will make a contribution to the economic life of the community, they will not be dependent on others for their maintenance.

Once we instill this attitude within our own students, we will need to work with other yeshivot to see if we can influence them in this direction as well. In particular, we need to devote tremendous effort to reshaping the way our girls are being taught in our schools. We must encourage girls to develop their own intellects and spirits. They must not see their primary goal as being subservient to the wishes of a husband who studies all day in a yeshiva. If the women learn to expect more of the men, the men will learn to expect more of themselves.

With a revamping of our system of *shidduchim,* we can help eliminate the unseemly materialistic elements in matchmaking. We can help relieve the financial strain on so many parents who feel they must support their married children. The current situation is unfair and irresponsible. It seems to me that it violates the ideals of the Torah.

Members of the Search Committee: I have taken up more than enough of your time. I apologize if I have gone on too long, but I feel that what I have told you is vital to your understanding of my husband and of me. I hope that this information will help you make the bold and creative decision to appoint my husband, Rav David Mercado, to the position of rosh yeshiva. Thank you.

Rabbi Shabsai Velt

MEMBERS OF THE SEARCH COMMITTEE: Thank you for inviting me to appear before you. As you know, I have been a teacher of Talmud in Yeshivas Lita for many, many years. I was a close friend and colleague of Rav Yosef Grossman, of blessed memory. I have known Rav Shimshon since he was a baby.

I also have gotten to know Rav David Mercado since he began studying in our yeshiva, and especially since he became a faculty member. I think I can give you a fair, honest evaluation of both men, from the perspective of someone who is a longtime teacher here.

Although I certainly have more seniority than either of these individuals, I know full well that I am not worthy of being a candidate for the office of rosh yeshiva. Indeed, I don't think any of the other rebbeim are suitable candidates either. So it comes down to an evaluation of Rav Shimshon and Rav Mercado.

Before I get to a discussion of the qualities of each candidate, let me preface my remarks with a short discourse on the contemporary challenges facing the Torah community. You know, as I know, that the Jewish people have had to struggle mightily throughout the generations in order to survive as a distinctive people. Since antiquity, we have been maligned, persecuted, and martyred for the sake of our religion. You also know, as I know, that we have not only faced threats to our physical existence, but we have also faced threats to our spiritual existence.

Hellenism, for example, was a dangerous phenomenon for our people during ancient times. Yes, the Hellenistic threat posed dangers to our lives, but it also sought to undermine our spirit. Hellenism was a culture steeped in paganism, idolatry, and reverence for the physical and material aspects of life. Its values came into clear conflict with the Jewish notions of monotheism, one incorporeal God, the primacy of the spiritual over the material. As long as Jews were united in their resistance to the Hellenistic teachings, we were able to be strong. When Jews began to assimilate into the Hellenistic culture, our people became fragmented. We were plagued with internal dissension and conflict.

We learned from the confrontation with Hellenism that Jews are better off when they remain faithful to their own ideals and teachings, when they are courageous enough to resist the temptations of assimilating into the dominant pagan culture. We would not be here today if it were up to the assimilationists. We are here only because of the total dedication and sacrifice of those Jews who heroically resisted the Hellenizing pressures.

During the nineteenth century, the Jewish people again faced a tremendous array of cultural pressures. The enlightened countries of Europe began to extend civil liberties and equal rights to Jews. In the United States, Jews had already attained political equality. The "gift" of political rights was a mixed blessing. On the one hand, it allowed Jews to rise in political, intellectual and economic life. Jews could now attend schools and universities which had previously been closed to them, or which had quotas limiting the number of Jewish students. So, from this perspective, freedom seemed to be a very good thing.

On the other hand, this very freedom was often bought at the price of our souls. Jews felt they needed to abandon Jewish laws and customs in order to fit in better with the non-Jewish society. Many gave up Judaism altogether. Many supported "reforms" in Judaism, reforms that essentially amounted to abandoning the commandments and traditions of Judaism. They wanted to be considered good Jews even if they worked on the Sabbath, ate pork, desecrated the festivals, and disregarded the laws of ritual purity.

The threat to the spiritual continuity of our people has been relentless. We must remember: the assimilationists and reformists have basically disappeared from Judaism. We are not their descendants. We are here because of a small, dedicated community of Jews who remained faithful to Torah at all costs, who resisted all the blandishments and temptations that the modern Western world had to offer.

Who will constitute the Jewish people fifty and one hundred years from now? They will be our children and grandchildren, not the descendants of the assimilationists and the reformists of our times. Those groups will be lost because they have cut themselves off from the Torah, the eternal tree of life. They have sold their souls for the sake of attaining material success in this world. A Jew without Torah is a body without a soul. The future generations of Jews will come only from Jews who are true to their souls and true to Torah.

We sometimes hear of the great achievements of Western civilization in general and of the greatness of America in particular. Certainly, Western culture has made outstanding technological progress. And certainly, it has produced some good and thoughtful people. But by and large, Western culture is a colossal failure in matters of the spirit.

The bankruptcy of Western civilization is amply demonstrated by twentieth-century Germany, which was the quintessential expression of Western culture. It produced great musicians, artists, writers, philosophers, and scientists. It was at the forefront – or so many thought – of an advanced and progressive civilization. And yet, this same Germany produced Hitler. Not only Hitler, but a nation of murderers and collaborators! With all their philosophy and art and science and music – they were still pagans, savages. Their so-called civilization was only a veneer. They were like the cat that turned into a princess, who fooled everyone until a mouse ran into the room. Then she showed she was still a cat. The Western world, with all its seeming charm and nobility, showed itself to be a particularly vicious cat.

And was it only Germany that succumbed to total evil? No. Germany had the active and passive assistance of all of Christian Europe. Even the United States did little to save the millions of Jews whose lives were snuffed out by the Nazis and their collaborators. Western civilization – if it can be called civilization at all – was shown in its true colors in the Nazi concentration camps, in the crematoria, in the gas chambers.

Think carefully. What progress has the Western world – and the Eastern world too for that matter – made in the area of morality and ethics? With all their material achievements, what has humanity gained spiritually from the past several thousand years? The answer is that humanity has made little progress. It is still quite pagan and primitive when it comes to the development of the human spirit.

The Jewish people, through our Torah, has given humanity the highest possible ideals. We have taught that the world was created by one God, and that all humanity descends from one couple, that all people are created in the image of God. The Talmud teaches, based on these Torah concepts, that all human beings essentially belong to one family, that we all have responsibilities to each other, that each life is unique and universal. Whatever moral progress has been made in the Western world has come from our Bible and from our religious teachings. Christianity and Islam built their edifices on a Jewish foundation. When they grew numerous and powerful, they pushed aside the spiritual teachings of the Torah. Instead, they built countries and civilizations based on violence, war, lust for power, greed, and savage oppression of dissidents. To this day, the Christian and Muslim nations have not attained the spiritual, moral and ethical heights delineated in our own Jewish tradition. Can it honestly be said that we can gain spiritually by adhering to their cultures? Aren't we much better off studying the only true fountain of truth, the Torah?

When it comes to materialism and technological innovation, the Western world is quite successful. They use their talents and energies to produce more luxuries for themselves, not to advance their spirits. They exploit the natural world for whatever treasures they can use for their own purposes.

We live in the United States, the powerful leader of the Western world. What are the outstanding achievements of America? We have many nuclear weapons so that we can destroy the entire world several times over! We have a society riddled with racial and religious discrimination, exploitation of the poor, low-quality public school education. American culture – if it may be called culture – is mired in hedonism and sexual license. Has all the material prosperity made America a land of righteousness, a land of moral integrity, a land of people striving to come closer to Godliness? No, not at all. While there are good people in America, the dominant culture is destructive toward spirituality, purity, and holiness.

This being the case, we need to think carefully. What strategy should the Torah community adopt in order to maintain its spiritual integrity? There is no point in studying Western civilization – it is morally bankrupt. There is no point in confronting American culture head on – it is too vast and pervasive. We can only be sullied by such a confrontation.

Moses Maimonides, our great medieval Torah luminary, provided an answer for us. He wrote that a Jew must live in a Torah environment. If his environment is inimical to Torah values, he should move to a better place. And if there is no better place, he should go off alone and live in the wilderness if necessary. In other words, our first and only quest in life is to live in an environment that fosters our religious growth and spiritual development. All sacrifices must be made to attain this goal.

In the modern world, there seems to be no place for us to hide. We are assaulted by radios and televisions and computers, by newspapers and magazines, by advertisements at bus stops. Immorality and promiscuity are all-encompassing, whether here or any other place in the Western world. So where can we flee? Where is our wilderness where we may live in isolation, free from the impurity that surrounds us?

Members of the Search Committee, the only haven for us in this day and age is the yeshiva and the community that surrounds and supports it. That is all we have. Our yeshiva is a fortress, a bastion of purity in a world of decadence.

When Yeshivas Lita was founded by Rav Leibel Grossman, his goal was to create a *mekom Torah* in America. He wanted to draw on the vast spiritual traditions that he had absorbed in the yeshivos of Poland and Lithuania. He saw that America was a spiritual wasteland and probably would remain a spiritual wasteland. He knew that he had to establish a Torah institution that would protect our teachings and traditions.

What is our yeshiva? It is an oasis in a spiritual desert. It is a place for young men to spend years in intensive Torah study. Here they can imbibe the pure, unsullied traditions of our people. Here they can develop their spirits and come closer to God. Here they can observe our commandments and customs in a safe and secure environment. Here they can live in an idyllic world that shuts out the filth and stridency of the outside world. Here they can become "married" to the Torah.

Our strategy, then, is most reasonable and responsible. I think that we are a good model not just for the Jewish people, but for idealistic non-Jews who want to maintain their ideals and standards. In this generation, everyone who wishes to serve God must necessarily go into exile. I hope and pray that the situation will improve in coming generations. Meanwhile, we must do all we can to preserve ourselves until better times arrive.

If the strategy I laid out is correct, our next step is to determine who would be best to lead our yeshiva in this spirit. Who is able to maintain our strength, our devotion, our love of God? Who is able to keep our yeshiva as a safe haven for pure and idealistic souls? Who is able to exact the highest standards of Torah study? Who can build the highest walls around our yeshiva so that we do not become contaminated by the evils of the outside world? Who can be the general in charge of our fortress?

Let me begin by saying who it cannot be. It cannot be Rav David Mercado.

I know him well. I know his strengths, I know his weaknesses. Yes, he is an impressive Torah scholar. Yes, he is enthusiastic, charismatic, and energetic. Yes, he is an inspiring and thoughtful teacher. Yes, he has genuine virtues.

But in spite of his talents, he simply does not share the philosophy of our yeshiva. He does not fully realize the dangers of the outside world, the seductive powers of the materialism and hedonism of American culture. He is naïve. He has studied a few years in college and feels that he is better for it. He does not realize, though, that his experience is the exception to the rule, not the rule. If all our yeshiva students had been enrolled in college, they would very likely not be the pious Torah scholars that they are. Many would have been corrupted in faith and deed. Many would have been lost to Torah and to our people.

I can see that students who have spent a year or more in Rav Mercado's classes have been infected with a certain skepticism. They are not heretics, Heaven forbid, but they are not truly pious anymore either. They question the authority of our sages. They are critical of the pedagogical methods of our yeshiva. In so many ways, obvious and subtle, they absorb the ideas and attitudes of Rav Mercado. They become restless and questioning. What is worse, they begin to study secular texts that Rav Mercado himself recommends to them.

In its first stages, this sort of intellectualism – or may I call it pseudo-intellectualism – seems innocuous enough. At worst, it is annoying to other students and other teachers. As this tendency progresses, though, it inevitably will lead to unrest in our yeshiva. There will be demands to change our curriculum and methods. There will be demands to introduce secular studies or to allow students to take courses in colleges, and there will be an increase in dissatisfaction and frustration. This will lead to a rift in the yeshiva. We have not arrived yet at the full impact of such a rift, but we can see that it will come if it is not stopped now. Unfortunately, and it pains me to say this, Rav Mercado is part of the problem, not part of the solution. For all his many virtues, he is a grave danger to the continued strength of Yeshivas Lita. He, like Aaron's unfortunate sons, is offering a strange fire, a fire that God has not requested. The ultimate result of this behavior is calamity.

It is not just that Rav Mercado is a maverick and a troublemaker. His wife does not fit into our pattern of life either. Both he and she are outsiders. They do not understand who we really are and what our goals really are. They do not understand the implication of their words and behavior.

I was a close friend of Rav Yosef Grossman, as you all know. On more than one occasion, I raised my concerns about Rav Mercado. Rav Yosef, may his memory be a blessing, recognized the problems, but somehow could not bring himself to discipline or release Rav Mercado. Why? Rav Yosef was excited by the new wonder-boy of our yeshiva. Here was a young man who had attended university, who had lived in the outside world, who chose to attend Yeshivas Lita of his own free will. Rav Yosef saw in David Mercado a fulfillment of a great hope, a hope that our yeshiva would be such a powerful intellectual and spiritual magnet that it would draw students who had not been raised in our system of schools. When Mercado made such phenomenal progress in his studies, Rav Yosef was delirious with joy. "You see," he told me, "it is possible to create new Rabbi Akivas even in our own days in America."

He was so astounded by Mercado's gifts that he simply overlooked Mercado's weaknesses. I told him: "Our yeshiva is not a hospital. It is not a place for sick, unhealthy souls. We only want students from sound backgrounds who have attended sound religious schools before coming here. We do not want or need students who are 'seekers of truth' who come from diluted religious backgrounds." Rav Yosef, though, was adamant. "I know that what you say is true," he told me, "but David Mercado proves that another point of view is also possible. Two opposing arguments can both be true. Both are the words of the living God."

When Mercado married a woman by the name of Sultana, the yeshiva community was scandalized. A student of our yeshiva arranged his own marriage? A student of our yeshiva married a woman who had not been raised in a religious Jewish home? The rumor went out – but was not verified – that Mercado's wife was a proselyte, who had been raised among non-Jews, who had attended church! Members of the Search Committee, even the most liberal of you must realize that this situation is outrageous, a stigma on the good name of Yeshivas Lita.

I again met with Rav Yosef to express my deep concerns about the propriety of keeping Mercado as a student in our yeshiva. Rav Yosef, a calm expression on his wise face, informed me that he not only wanted Mercado to continue as a student here, but he also had invited Mercado to become a teacher in our yeshiva. When I protested, Rav Yosef replied: "Rav Shabsai, we have known each other for many years. You think I am making a mistake. Perhaps I am, perhaps I am not. I see in this young man a spark of genius and originality that I have not seen in many years. I see him and his wife as symbols of the victory of our yeshiva and our methods. We have succeeded in drawing these two very unlikely candidates into our world. If they succeed here, perhaps we will be able to draw many more like them. There are many seekers of truth among our people scattered throughout America. We should want them to be drawn to our world. The Mercados prove that we can succeed in reaching the best and brightest Jews, regardless of where they grew up and how they were educated."

"But they may be a negative influence," I persisted.

"To make a fine loaf of bread, you need a little yeast. The yeast looks bad and smells bad, but it stirs things up. It generates good bread."

"But yeast is *chometz*. *Chometz* can have a bad connotation!"

"Rav Shabsai," he said with a laugh, "you leave the *chometz* in this yeshiva to me."

As the years passed and Mercado's influence among students grew, it became clear that he was stirring up trouble. He may not have intended to create dissension, but it was an inevitable result of his style. Even so, Rav Yosef tolerated him. "A little excitement is good," he would say.

In spite of Rav Yosef's obvious affection for Mercado, I am sure he would never have wanted that man to become rosh yeshiva. I don't think he ever considered such a possibility. He wanted Mercado here as a symbol of the yeshiva's intellectual power. He liked the excitement Mercado created because he felt this would attract intellectual young Jews – and, in fact, it has attracted bright new students. It is one thing to tolerate a person as a teacher, and an altogether different thing to appoint him as the rosh yeshiva. I can assure you, knowing Rav Yosef as well as I did, that he would not for a moment want Mercado to succeed him as rosh yeshiva. He knew that Mercado lacked the credibility and stature to head our yeshiva.

This brings us to Rav Shimshon. I am certain that Rav Yosef had every expectation that his son would take over as rosh yeshiva. It is a pity – a tragedy – that Rav Yosef died suddenly and was unable to express his wishes for the future of our yeshiva. We may be sure, though, that he would have appointed his own beloved and worthy son, Rav Shimshon.

I have known Rav Shimshon since he was a baby. I have seen him grow into the outstanding scholar that he is today. From his childhood, he had one goal and one goal only: to master Torah. He studied day and night. He memorized page after page. He was the most diligent student I have ever seen. Rav Yosef doted on him.

When Rav Shimshon received *semikha* from his father, the entire yeshiva had a day of celebration. All of us – old and young – knew that the chain of tradition of our yeshiva was extended. We saw in the young Rav Shimshon a future *godol hador*, an able and worthy successor to his father, in due course.

Rav Shimshon has lived up to our expectations. He is widely respected for the thoroughness of his Torah scholarship. Few people in this generation can match his mastery of Talmud and commentaries. He is regarded as a leading authority in matters of Jewish law. He has devoted his life to studying and teaching Torah in this yeshiva. It is no secret that he always expected to become the rosh yeshiva. To deprive him of this title would be, if I may say so, unjust and immoral. To deprive the yeshiva of his leadership would be tragic.

Rav Shimshon is fully cognizant of the dangers of the outside world. He knows that our yeshiva is a fortress in the wilderness. He is committed to strengthening our bastion of Torah.

Members of the Search Committee, as a long-standing faculty member of our yeshiva I urge you to appoint Rav Shimshon Grossman as our rosh yeshiva as soon as possible. Every day of delay is a day lost. Yeshivas Lita will thrive and prosper under the able leadership of Rav Shimshon.

Rav Hazkel Gottlieb

MEMBERS OF THE SEARCH COMMITTEE: I appear before you as a member of the faculty of our yeshiva for the past ten years. Thank you for allowing me to make my presentation.

I want to tell you frankly that I am frightened about what is happening in our yeshiva and in the Torah world in general. I believe with all my heart that we have the right intentions, the right talents, but that we have veered away from the true path.

Rav Shimshon, may he live and be well, is fond of referring to the story of Rabbi Yosei ben Kisma. Rabbi Yosei turned down an offer of a huge fortune rather than to leave his enclave of Torah scholars. According to Rav Shimshon, this proves that we must not be enticed away from the safety and security of our Torah community. We must turn away every offer and every consideration. Nothing is more important than living in a community of Torah scholars.

Rav Mercado has commented on this story many times. He has pointed out an obvious question: if all Torah scholars were to adopt the attitude of Rabbi Yosei ben Kisma, who would teach Torah to the millions of Jews who do not live in Torah centers? What would happen to the religious lives of all those Jews who do not live within the precincts of a great yeshiva? In fact, says Rav Mercado, Rabbi Yosei's attitude was defeatist, self-centered, and destructive to the overall welfare of the Jewish people. Rabbi Yosei looked out for his own spiritual welfare, but showed inadequate concern for the welfare of others. Perhaps if he had accepted the man's offer, he would have been able to influence an entire community for the good. He might have helped many souls come closer to the teachings of Torah.

Rav Mercado noted that the very next passage in the Mishnah, right after the story of Rabbi Yosei ben Kisma, teaches that the Almighty has five possessions in this world. The first one is Torah, but Torah is only one of the possessions. The next is heaven and earth. In order to come closer to God, we need to have a grand view of His creation. Our minds need to span heaven and earth. Another of God's possessions is Abraham. Abraham was distinguished by his concern for others, his hospitality to friends and strangers alike. Rabbinic tradition teaches that Abraham and Sarah spent much time and effort speaking to pagans, bringing them to an understanding of God, converting them into God-fearing and God-loving people. Abraham certainly did not share the view of Rabbi Yosei ben Kisma! Another of God's possessions is Israel. From this we learn that we must have a commitment to all the people of Israel, to the land of Israel. Israel was chosen by God not to be an exclusive, self-enclosed nation, but to be a light unto the nations, to spread the ideas and ideals of Torah to the world at large. To accomplish this, we must repudiate the isolationist philosophy of Rabbi Yosei ben Kisma. Another of God's possessions is the Beit ha-Mikdash, the Holy Temple that stood in Jerusalem in ancient times. The Beit ha-Mikdash was, of course, a place of worship for the people of Israel. But it also was the place where Israel brought offerings for the welfare of all the nations of the world!

The Beit ha-Mikdash represents the values of compassion and loving-kindness. Rabbinic tradition has it that the Beit ha-Mikdash was built on the place where two brothers met on a certain night. The story is as follows. The brothers owned a farm together. One of the brothers was married and had children. The other brother was unmarried and lived alone. At the end of the harvest, the brothers divided the crop evenly, each one taking his half of the produce.

In the middle of the night, the married brother awoke. He said to himself: I am blessed with a good wife who cooks and cleans and sews. My brother, though, is a bachelor. He must pay people to do this work for him. He needs more money than I do. So the brother went outside, loaded his wagon with produce, and started to go to his brother's house. His plan was to put this produce next to his brother's produce, without his brother ever realizing that he had gotten the extra amount.

At the same time, the bachelor brother awoke. He said to himself: I am a single man, I have few expenses. My brother, though, must support a wife and children. He needs more money than I do. So the brother went outside, loaded his wagon with produce, and started to go to his brother's house. His plan was to put this produce next to his brother's produce, without his brother ever realizing that he got the extra amount.

As the two brothers, filled with love and compassion for each other, rushed to deliver their goods, their wagons met on the road. They both realized what they were up to. They embraced in brotherly love. At that very spot, says the rabbinic tradition, the Beit ha-Mikdash was eventually built. It was constructed on a foundation of love, empathy, and concern for others.

Rav Mercado explained that the passage of the five possessions of God was placed there as a chastisement to Rabbi Yosei ben Kisma. It insisted that our religion demands a wide range of concerns and commitments. To be true to the message of Torah, we must look outward, not just inward.

Nearly thirty-five hundred years ago, God revealed the Ten Commandments to the children of Israel at Mount Sinai. This awesome revelation, unique in human history, was a spiritual high point for all humanity. It never happened before or since that an entire nation, numbering perhaps two million souls, experienced the presence of God in such a direct manner. That revelation was to change the course of human history as no other event has ever done. The people of Israel were charged with teaching Godliness and morality to the nations of the world.

This was a tremendous burden for God to have placed on the shoulders of one small people. We have carried this burden throughout the centuries and have, in fact, made remarkable contributions to human civilization. We have paid a heavy price, and we have suffered abuse, scorn and persecution, but we have never lost sight of our responsibility to all nations, even those that have sought our destruction.

We have been able to accomplish much because – in spite of antagonism toward us – we have not been afraid. We have confronted every culture boldly and courageously. No people on the face of this earth has shown the consistent spiritual fortitude of the Jewish people, generation after generation, for thousands of years.

In our days, though, I am afraid that the ascending philosophy in the Torah world calls for isolationism. It assumes that we will lose too many souls if we confront modern culture. It assumes that we are too weak, too small. It sees our task today as building fortresses in which we may hide, protected from the influences of the outside world. This is the philosophy of our yeshiva and of many other yeshivot. It is a philosophy of cowardice and weakness!

Can we imagine that God took the trouble to reveal His glory to us at Mount Sinai only so that we would later confine ourselves to our own neighborhoods and self-imposed ghettos? Can it be that this was the ultimate intention of His choosing the people of Israel – that we should live outside the mainstream of society, confined to our own four cubits? It should be absurd to say so. Yet I am afraid that our yeshiva – and the world it represents – is working under this dangerous and foolish assumption. It is dedicated to being a self-enclosed community.

The Torah was not given to us so that we should study it in a vacuum. It was given to us as a forthright challenge by God. We are to study Torah so that we may apply its lessons to the real world, so that we may lift all the people of the world to a deeper understanding of the One God, of morality, of spiritual growth. We cannot accomplish these things if all we do is talk to ourselves!

Rav Mercado has dared to articulate an open, courageous and outward-looking philosophy. He has dared to challenge the unstated assumptions that have taken root in the Torah world, assumptions of isolationism and insularity. Rav Yosef appreciated the message of Rav Mercado, even though Rav Yosef was too steeped in the old school to call for necessary changes. He was content to let Rav Mercado stir things up.

Look at our yeshiva and the other yeshivot that are part of our world. The students – almost to a one – dress identically. They wear white shirts, black suits, black hats with broad brims. Most of them look deprived of sunlight; they are wan and sallow from an indoor life of study. The conformity in costume is an outer reflection of conformity in thought. They learn very early what they may believe and what they may not believe, what they may say and what they may not say, what they may ask and what they may not ask. They learn that they must submit to authority and that they may never take issue with the opinions of our great sages.

This overwhelming pressure toward conformity is destructive of the human spirit and the human intellect. The greatest sages in the past achieved greatness precisely because they had wide latitude in their thinking, because they were encouraged to think independently and creatively. The more room we give our students to think and to explore, the more likely it is that they will achieve greatness.

Rav Shimshon and those of his ilk claim that we live in a generation where freedom of thought and expression must be severely curtailed. They say that the outside society is so filled with evil temptations we can only survive by walking a straight and narrow path. They are afraid of freedom and nonconformity. Yet although there is some basis for their fears, isn't there even more basis for fear in the other direction? If we do not foster openness and intellectual curiosity, do we not run the risk of turning Torah Judaism into a narrow sect rather than being a world religion? Do we not run the risk of ossification, of making Judaism a fossil from antiquity rather than a living force in the world?

Rav Mercado often stresses that Jews are, after all, human beings. As human beings, we should have a natural interest in all human civilization. The non-Jews of the world are also our brothers and sisters. All of us were created in the image of God. We should want to learn from all people, from the best that all human civilizations have produced. Nothing human should be alien to us.

Our yeshiva now has the opportunity to make a dramatic change. We can move in a new direction, and we can influence other yeshivot to redirect themselves as well. By selecting Rav Mercado as our rosh yeshiva, you will be giving an important signal to the entire Torah world. You will be saying: Yeshivat Lita is not afraid of intellectual freedom and open discourse. It is not afraid of unpopular ideas. It is not afraid of the outside world. Yeshivat Lita is confident that the Torah can stand up to every culture and to every challenge. We can take that which is good in external culture and leave behind the chaff. We can learn from all people. We can develop Torah personalities who are deeply steeped in Torah learning, but who are also comfortable and fearless in their confrontation with the world.

Our yeshiva can set the example for our generation and generations yet to come, teaching that Judaism must and can interact successfully with the cultures of the world. We have not forgotten the challenge and responsibility of the revelation at Mount Sinai.

By selecting Rav Mercado, you will be moving our yeshiva in a new, creative and dynamic direction. We can hope for much greatness to emerge from our yeshiva.

If you choose Rav Shimshon, then, in my humble opinion, you will lock our yeshiva into its regressive pattern. You will insure that yet another generation of Torah students will be raised in a spirit of isolation, fearfulness, ignorance of the world, conformism. You will pull the Torah into narrower and narrower confines.

To be honest, I think it is a positive sign that we have a search committee in the first place. Many people had simply assumed that Rav Shimshon would be appointed rosh yeshiva without any discussion or process of interviews. You, Members of the Search Committee, are to be commended, along with all the members of the board of trustees of our yeshiva. The fact that you had the gumption to create this committee and to insist that it operate independently – this alone is a monumental achievement.

But the fear is this: do you really have a voice in the future of our yeshiva? Is your committee truly independent, or are you merely going through the motions of democratic process in order to appease some malcontents?

Members of the Search Committee, here is an opportunity for you to find your voice, to make a bold decision, to make a commitment to freedom and creativity rather than to authoritarianism and conformity. Please, let us hear your voice. Let us hear your voice loud and clear.

Shammai Abelson

MEMBERS OF THE SEARCH COMMITTEE: As a longtime student of Yeshivas Lita, I want to share some of my thoughts with you about our yeshiva. I hope my words will be useful to you in your deliberations.

I grew up in a religious neighborhood in Brooklyn. My father and mother were both very strict in their religious observance. When I was five years old, they enrolled me in a yeshiva elementary school in our neighborhood. I attended that yeshiva until high school, when I was enrolled in a very strict yeshiva high school also in our neighborhood. When I was eighteen, I began my studies here at Yeshivas Lita, and I have been here for the past ten years. When I will leave, Heaven knows! I hope not too soon! I love this yeshiva more than I can say. It is a home – more than a home – to me.

Our yeshiva has two dorms. One is for single students, where I lived for my first three years. The other is for married students, where I lived for the next three years. Once we had our second child, though, the dorm facilities could not accommodate our family. So we moved into a nearby apartment building, where our yeshiva has arranged for a number of apartments for married students with larger families.

I tell you these things because they indicate how deeply concerned our yeshiva is with the wellbeing of students. Our yeshiva is more than an academic institution – it is an extended family, and it wants to keep all of its students comfortably housed in the yeshiva's orbit. Even students whose parents live nearby are not allowed to live at home. No. They, too, must live in the yeshiva's housing. The yeshiva creates its own world. It tolerates no distractions.

This is a powerful and wonderful thing. It creates a communal solidarity that is hard to put into words. The students get to know each other quite well, we become like one family. The older students take an interest in helping the younger students.

We get to know fairly early which students are the most serious, the most compassionate, the most learned. We also get to know which students are the laziest, the most selfish, the least learned. To a stranger looking at the students, we all look pretty much the same. But from the inside, we can distinguish the various characteristics – positive and negative – about each of our fellow students. Whatever character traits exist in humanity, we can observe them all from within the precincts of the yeshiva.

The most important room of the yeshiva is the Beis Medrash, the study hall. I remember the first time I entered the Beis Medrash of Yeshivas Lita: chills ran up my spine. I had never witnessed anything more powerful or more thrilling.

The Beis Medrash is a huge room. It has five rows of tables, fifteen deep, with room for eight students at each table. When the

Beis Medrash is full, which is from early morning until late into the night, it is a sight straight from the World to Come. It is so far above anything in this world that it is the closest we can come to heaven while still living on earth!

The Beis Medrash roars with the song of Torah study. At each table, small groups of students pore over the text of the Talmud. They analyze, discuss, argue. They search the commentaries for insights and explanations. The din in the room, far from disturbing concentration, is the sweetest background music. Each of us thinks better when we hear the voices of our fellow students – the more, the louder, the better.

So the first impression of the full Beis Medrash is that of density: hundreds of students in close proximity, each trying to fathom the meanings and mysteries of the sacred texts. Along with the sense of density, we have the incredible noise, the noise that sounds like the churning of a great machine. This noise is beautiful beyond description.

The Beis Medrash is distinguished by other characteristics besides its hugeness, its density, its noise. We see that the walls are lined with bookcases, and the bookcases are crammed with books. Students borrow the books freely when they need to refer to them, and then return them to the shelves. What are these books? The Talmud, Maimonides, the great Talmudic commentaries of our medieval sages of Spain, France, Italy and Germany, the codes of Jewish law compiled by Rabbi Yaakov ben Asher and Rabbi Joseph Karo, and books of rabbinic responsa.

For us, the students in the Beis Medrash, these books are like living human beings. We turn to them as we would turn to wise friends and learned teachers. We feel that we know them. We hear their voices. We read the words of the sages who lived in many lands over many eras, but they are all our contemporaries. Their words are alive. They participate actively in our discussions and debates.

The Beis Medrash, then, is a taste of the World to Come where all the great sages sit together, with crowns on their heads, to study Torah in the presence of God. In our Beis Medrash, we transcend time, we transcend life and death. We participate not only in the community of fellow students, but in the community of the Torah sages of all previous generations.

We notice something else in the Beis Medrash. At the front of the room, against the east wall, are stands – *shtenders* – and small tables reserved for our rebbeim, our teachers of Talmud and Jewish law. The rebbeim study with as much eagerness and intensity as their students. They are available to help students when difficult questions arise or when the meaning of a text is unclear. The rebbeim spend long hours studying, sometimes alone, sometimes with each other.

When we look at the rebbeim, we see our teachers and our guides. We see men who have achieved vast Torah knowledge, who are thoroughly devoted to studying, who strive to grow greater and greater in their learning. The rebbeim are not only our teachers and halakhic authorities. They are our inspiration. They show us what we, too, may attain if we are diligent enough in our studies. There is nothing higher or more wonderful in this world than to be a rebbe in an advanced yeshiva such as ours. Very few of us students will achieve that level, but many of us will become teachers of Torah on the high-school or elementary-school levels. This, too, is the work of Heaven.

The Beis Medrash has another very important feature: it has no windows. No windows!

When we are studying in the Beis Medrash, we cannot look out a window to see if it is day or night. We cannot tell if we are in New York or Jerusalem or Paris. We cannot take a break by looking at what is going on outside. The Beis Medrash transcends time and place.

In the Beis Medrash, I feel whole and pure. I feel a profound sense of belonging to the eternal people of Israel. As I struggle over passages of Talmud with my fellow students, I feel that – in some mystical way – I am in the presence of God. I think that all my fellow students feel this special inspiration.

I don't think that students in universities have this feeling. I don't think people in business have this feeling. But I know that yeshiva students feel that they are doing God's work on earth, that they are coming as close to God as is possible for any human being. The Beis Medrash is not just a place for intellectual striving. It is a holy sanctuary for our souls and spirits. The Beis Medrash is the place where we learn and grow, struggle and achieve, gain knowledge and come closer to God. Where else in the world is there such a place as the Beis Medrash?

We normally say our morning prayers in the Beis Medrash at 6:30 a.m. After a quick breakfast at the dorm cafeteria, we return to the Beis Medrash as soon as we can in order to get into our studies. We break again for lunch at about noon. At one o'clock, many of the students attend the classes given by our rebbeim. Some of the more advanced students, though, remain in the Beis Medrash and continue studying on their own. One of the rebbeim stays in the Beis Medrash to guide and assist these students.

While each of the rebbeim has his own particular style, the general approach of the classes is as follows: one of the students is called upon to read the text of Talmud that the class is studying. The rebbe then asks a series of questions about the text. Students offer answers by quoting from commentaries or by making suggestions of their own. More questions are asked. More discussion follows. Students then ask questions. The rebbe answers. He cites parallel texts in the Talmud, points out discrepancies, and offers resolutions to the questions. We might spend nearly two hours studying five or six lines of Talmud. But each word of these lines is scrutinized from every possible angle. This process helps us to learn how to think, how to see distinctions, how to reconcile contradictions. It also teaches us patience. It is fine and proper to spend several hours studying a few lines of Talmud. We are in no rush. If we study a few lines thoroughly each and every day, eventually we will cover a lot of ground and we will know the material well.

Rav Shimshon is a master at getting students to analyze texts. He is so well versed in Talmud and commentaries that he can draw questions and comparisons from the vast corpus of rabbinic literature. He detects analogies from one text to another, he sees connections where we would never have seen them. Among students, he is known as the best hair-splitter in the yeshiva. He makes distinctions, and distinctions to the distinctions, and then yet more distinctions. He can virtually split hairs.

I have been a student in Rav Shimshon's classes for the past three years. I am in awe of his knowledge. He has so much information at his fingertips. You ask him a question, and he knows the answer long before you have had the chance to finish your question.

Rav Shimshon is by far the most erudite of our rebbeim, as far as the students are concerned. Students are amazed by his memory, his agility of mind, his thorough knowledge.

I suppose it is no secret that most students assume that Rav Shimshon will be our next rosh yeshiva. He will make a wonderful rosh yeshiva. He will keep our yeshiva as it is and as it has been – a place totally dedicated to Torah, a place that resembles the World to Come.

Rav Shimshon is a tyrant when it comes to the issue of wasting time. He has no tolerance for nonsense. He chastises us frequently about the sin of wasting time. After all, time is the most precious gift that the Almighty has given us. We only have a limited and irreplaceable quantity at our disposal. A minute wasted is a minute lost forever. It is a minute that should have been spent studying Torah or fulfilling the precepts of the Torah. Rav Shimshon scorns the popular American phrase "killing time." Do we really have time to "kill"? Is time of so little value to us that we can squander it on foolishness and vanity? Americans will sit for hours viewing a baseball game, or watching television, or drinking at a bar. They waste, they "kill" their time, because they do not fully appreciate the sanctity of time. They do not realize how precious it is. They fritter away their lives, minute by minute, hour by hour, day by day. At the end, what do they have to show for their lives? They have forfeited the opportunity to develop their spirits and their minds, and they have given themselves to "killing" time. Those who "kill" time are in fact guilty of "killing" themselves, destroying their own souls.

Rav Shimshon is a no-nonsense person. He knows the truth, he teaches the truth, and he has little patience for those who stray from the true path. He has lived his entire life in the world of our yeshiva. He has grown up in the purity and holiness of our Beis Medrash. His hair has turned gray in the precincts of Torah. He is on a loftier level than most others, who have not been so fortunate to live their lives in such a holy environment.

Some years ago, I was a student in Rav David Mercado's class. Let me say at once that Rav Mercado does appreciate the incredible power and pull of the Beis Medrash. No one can accuse him of not spending many long hours in Torah study. He has proven himself to be a worthy scholar and teacher of Torah. I enjoyed being in his class.

That is the problem with him. I *enjoyed* being in his class. I cannot say that about my years in Rav Shimshon's class. Rav Shimshon's classes are work. They make us sweat and squirm, and push us to our limits. But Rav Mercado – his classes may be said to be enjoyable.

Rav Mercado peppers his classes with stories, humorous comments, discussions of secular books that he has found of value. He introduces students to many new ideas, ideas that are not heard anywhere else within the walls of our yeshiva. Yes, we study the talmudic texts, but we do so in the spirit of enjoyment, as though we were trying to solve a puzzle or a riddle. He eggs us on, teases us, laughs with us. Students, of course, enjoy his classes and learn a great deal, but because of his familiar style with students, he does not command the same respect and prestige as Rav Shimshon. Students revere Rav Shimshon, they like Rav Mercado. That is a big difference!

Rav Mercado tries to have his students attain the clearest and simplest understanding of the text. If Rav Shimshon is a hairsplitter, Rav Mercado despises *pilpul* and intellectual gymnastics.

With Rav Shimshon, the Talmud shows itself to be a storehouse of complications and contradictions needing ingenious explication. With Rav Mercado, the Talmud shows itself to be a storehouse of legal and ethical discussion requiring relatively simple clarification.

When asked about his approach to Talmud, Rav Mercado once gave the following answer. Let us say that a scholar today becomes the world's foremost expert of Ptolemaic astronomy. He knows all the mathematical formulae, all the rotations and orbits of the heavenly bodies exactly as taught by Ptolemy. Some people would say that he was a great scholar, the best in the world. He has mastered a difficult body of knowledge better than anyone else. But I would say that this scholar has wasted his time. He is essentially a fool. Why? Because Ptolemy's system has been shown to be incorrect. Every schoolchild today knows more true astronomy than this scholar of the Ptolemaic system who still believes the earth is the center of the universe. Thus, just because a person has great mastery over a particular subject does not mean in and of itself that he is wise. If he is working with the wrong assumptions, his conclusions will also be wrong. He is wasting time and effort by using discredited methods and incorrect facts. My goal in studying Talmud is to get to the truth using the best methods. Usually, the least complicated and most direct route is the way to reach the correct result. The more convoluted the reasoning is, the more likely that the whole process is incorrect.

In effect, then, Rav Mercado is discrediting Rav Shimshon and the tradition that he symbolizes. He compares Rav Shimshon to a scholar of Ptolemaic astronomy. Of course, this is utter nonsense. Rav Mercado is wrong to level such an accusation against Rav

Shimshon, who is recognized by many to be one of the Torah giants of our generation.

I will tell you honestly: it is difficult to go from Rav Mercado's class to the class of any other of the rebbeim, including Rav Shimshon. The difference between him and the others is like the difference between diamonds and coal. He is luminous, multifaceted, brilliant.

So why, you may ask, did I transfer out of Rav Mercado's class into Rav Shimshon's? I did so because I believe Rav Shimshon is more authentic, that he represents the traditions of this yeshiva more completely. Even if his style is more ponderous and onerous, this is the way students have been taught in Yeshivas Lita for the past several generations and the way they were taught in Eastern Europe for many generations before. The fact is, this system works! Generations of Torah scholars have followed this pattern. It is tempting to change directions now, but it is an evil temptation. We are obviously doing things right. We have a yeshiva full of students, with many more students waiting for the opportunity to study here. We have the most incredible Beis Medrash, the most intense Torah learning. Our way of life is thriving.

In every generation, there are people who come up with new-fangled ideas and strategies. They try to innovate, but their innovations are rejected. Why are they rejected? Because accepting those innovations costs too much! It means changing our pattern, uprooting our stability, undermining our certainty. By following the time tested traditional system, we survive and flourish. By running after every new idea, we simply flounder and lose our way.

Rav Mercado, let me assure you, is not a rebel or a revolutionary. I am quite sure that he would want to maintain the qualities that have made our yeshiva so strong. But things would not be the same if he were to become the rosh yeshiva. Small cracks would start to appear in the spiritual structure of Yeshivas Lita. At first they might seem barely noticeable, harmless. With the passage of time, they will open up into large breaches. Once the equanimity and harmony of the Beis Medrash is broken, it will be impossible to restore or repair.

So, although I like Rav Mercado very much, I think he would not be suitable as our rosh yeshiva. His intentions would be good, his dedication would be unquestioned, but the results of his efforts will be to destroy the yeshiva as we know it. He might not intend this to happen, but it will surely happen.

Rav Shimshon is the natural and right choice for rosh yeshiva of Yeshivas Lita. He is solid as a rock. He is a fortress. He cannot be moved. He will hold things together in the tradition of his father and grandfather, and his ancestors going back to the great yeshivos of Eastern Europe. With Rav Shimshon as rosh yeshiva, we will be able to sleep peacefully at night, knowing that no innovations and modern ideas will corrupt and undermine our age-old system. We will continue to bask in the glow of our yeshiva, which is surely a taste of heaven on earth.

Chaim Baruch Haber

MEMBERS OF THE SEARCH COMMITTEE: Thank you for inviting me to appear before you to discuss the future rosh yeshiva of our great institution of Torah learning. As you know, I am a devoted student of Rav David Mercado, and I have attended his classes for the past three years. I state at the outset that I think he would make an outstanding contribution to our yeshiva if he were appointed as rosh yeshiva.

It goes without saying that he is an erudite scholar and a brilliant teacher. Otherwise, you would not be considering his candidacy in the first place. So I do not wish to waste your time by telling you things that are already well known to you. Rather, I would like to talk about some of the qualities of Rav Mercado, qualities that distinguish him as an unusual human being and an extraordinary figure in the Torah world.

I came to Yeshivat Lita six years ago. I had previously studied in elementary and high school yeshivas in Brooklyn. My world was the world of yeshivas. My thoughts and dreams were encompassed by the world in which I lived. I chose to come to our yeshiva because of its fame as the leading academy of advanced Torah studies in America. It was a natural extension of the education I had received up to that point in my life.

My first three years here were spent in the classes of three different rebbeim. I learned much from each of them. Everything was just as I had expected it to be. But by the end of my third year, I was feeling that I had fallen into a rut. Every day seemed the same as the day before. Every tomorrow would no doubt be the same as today. I was treading water. I think many yeshiva students go through this stage; it is frustrating and depressing. I was feeling tired and lackadaisical. Nothing really excited my interest. I just plodded along in my studies, covered the texts I was supposed to cover – but with little enthusiasm.

I even considered leaving the yeshiva. I didn't see the point of continuing the tedium.

A fellow student, seeing my dismay, suggested that I enroll in the class of Rav Mercado. He told me that Rav Mercado was a different kind of person, a different kind of teacher. If anyone could rekindle the spark of enthusiasm within me, Rav Mercado was the one.

So I arranged to be placed in Rav Mercado's class, and decided to stay in the yeshiva for one more year. That decision changed my life. As you see, I have continued as a student in the yeshiva these past three years, and hope to spend another year in Rav Mercado's class before going out on my own as a teacher of Torah.

What impresses me about Rav Mercado? His classes are alive, challenging, fresh. He makes the discussions of Talmudic texts so interesting and so relevant that you begin to wonder how anyone in the world can get through life without having studied Talmud. He draws from so many sources of knowledge. In a typical class, for example, he will cite biographical information about the sages whose words are quoted in the text, the historical context of their words, and the history of the text itself. He will cite lessons from history, archeology, anthropology. He will discuss comparative issues in Babylonian and Roman legal systems. He will share fascinating insights from the fields of psychology and literature, and also will draw on scientific knowledge when relevant to the discussion at hand. The range of his reading is vast, and he stimulates us to do outside reading on our own.

Aside from his fascinating approach to Talmud and Jewish law, he also devotes time to issues in Jewish philosophy and contemporary Jewish life. He challenges us to examine and re-examine our various assumptions, and he tells us that we must each search for truth to the best of our abilities. When we ask him for a definitive answer to a question, his usual response is: What do you think? He encourages us to seek, to question, to offer answers of our own. He guides us with incredible wisdom. He prods us, encourages us, and helps us when we find ourselves stuck in an intellectual or emotional quagmire. He is patient, loving, and understanding. He is excited about ideas, and he conveys that excitement to his students.

Let me tell you: after having studied in yeshivas since my earliest childhood, I could never have imagined coming across a personality like Rav Mercado. He is more open, more imaginative, more committed to freedom of thought and expression than any teacher I have ever had. His classes cleanse the mind and strengthen the soul.

One of his central teachings is that we are human beings! This does not sound like such a revolutionary idea, but in the world of yeshivas, it really *is* revolutionary. We tend to see ourselves within the narrow confines of our Torah community. We generally speak only among ourselves and other like-minded people. It is as though the other billions of people in the world do not exist, or as though they have their world, we have ours, and we have no reason to want to interact with them. Rav Mercado reminds us that all human beings are created in the image of God and that we all are – essentially – part of one great human family. We have responsibilities to each other.

The interesting thing about Rav Mercado is that he doesn't just teach this idea – he puts its implications into practice. He is a member of the neighborhood community board, where he works together with other area leaders on projects of concern to the entire community. He is the only member of the yeshiva community to be a member of the community board. Can you imagine any of the other rebbeim or older students taking part in meetings together with people of different religions, races, backgrounds? Can you imagine Rav Shimshon participating in such a forum? No, of course not. Rav Mercado has a much broader and wider vision, rooted in a much deeper and more universal understanding of Torah Judaism. He teaches us that all human beings, including ourselves, are responsible to work for *yishuv olam,* the advancement of human life, human civilization.

Rav Mercado serves as chairman of the committee on medical ethics of the Federation of Jewish Philanthropies. He has become a world renowned expert in the field, not only because of his amazing halakhic and ethical knowledge, but also because he has spent many hours studying the modern technologies used in hospitals. He tells his students that to know Jewish law is to know more than texts. It is to know reality, the world as it is. And he puts this teaching into practice. He goes to conferences on medical ethics and participates actively in them. He shares his knowledge of Jewish tradition with other medical ethicists and learns from their research and insights. He has also become quite knowledgeable of the medical ethics teachings of other religions.

Who else in the Torah community plays such an active and influential role in the field of medical ethics? Who else is not only a brilliant theoretician, but an active participant in the ongoing discussions? Who else brings the vision of Torah to the larger community with such clarity and understanding?

By serving as chairman of the committee on medical ethics, Rav Mercado has taken a lot of criticism from members of the yeshiva world. The Federation, as you all know, is comprised of Jews of all religious points of view and, in fact, the Orthodox are a small minority of participants. The committee on medical ethics includes not only laymen, but also non-Orthodox rabbis. Many in the yeshiva world feel it is forbidden to sit together with non-Orthodox rabbis and organizations. All the more do they oppose sitting with them on committees that specifically relate to issues in Jewish law. What right do the non-Orthodox have to express opinions on medical ethics? After all, they don't even adhere to halakha! The Reform movement has denied the Divine nature of halakha! So, the critics say, Rav Mercado's participation on – and his chairmanship of – a committee that includes non-Orthodox members is an outrage! Rav Mercado gives them credibility by treating them as equals.

Rav Mercado is well aware of this criticism. On a number of occasions, he has discussed it with us in his classes. He respects the point of view of his critics, but believes that it is wrong-minded and antithetical to true Torah values. He asks: If the Federation of Jewish Philanthropies, which represents the interests of the large majority of Jews in our city, has a committee on medical ethics, should the Orthodox be there or not? Do the Orthodox think that they advance the cause of Torah by abstaining from participation? Do they think they fulfill God's will by isolating themselves from the rest of the Jewish public? The Federation exists, the committee on medical ethics exists, the committee is called upon to represent Jewish interests in many public forums, in hospitals, in conferences. Should the yeshiva world cede responsibility to those who have less knowledge of Torah than we, who have less commitment to Torah than we? It is ludicrous to think so. Our task is to deal with reality as it is, and to make our best efforts to move things in the proper direction. It is easy to be a righteous moralist within the walls of a yeshiva, but the true test of righteousness and morality is on the front lines, where the action is.

Precisely because Rav Mercado is respectful to others, he is also respected by them. He is able to accomplish important things for Torah by making the Torah beloved by the people with whom he interacts – even non-Jews, even non-Orthodox Jews. He became chairman of the Federation's committee because he won the respect of all the others. They recognized that his knowledge was far greater than theirs, that he represented an authentic Torah point of view. They defer to him because he respects and accepts them as fellow brothers and sisters. Does this imply in any way that he legitimates their religious perspectives? Of course not! When he participates as a member of the community board, he sits with people of different backgrounds and religions. Does this mean that he legitimates their religious and political philosophies? Of course not! Working with people of different beliefs does not imply acceptance of their beliefs. It merely implies the recognition that we are all human beings trying to work together for the common good.

Rav Mercado has encouraged his students to do volunteer work in the community. I myself have worked at a homeless shelter during the winter months. Some people say that this is a waste of time. The hours spent in such service should have been spent studying Torah! Every minute away from the Beit Midrash is a minute lost forever! Rav Mercado, though, believes that community service is a way of fulfilling the Torah lessons that we study in class and in the Beit Midrash. He makes the following analogy: let us say that a person studies the art of swimming. He learns the strokes and techniques – but he never sets foot in the water! Can such a person be described as a swimmer? Surely he knows all there is to know about the art of swimming, but he does not know how to swim! He must get into the water and adapt his classroom learning to reality. Would anyone say that a student of swimming is wasting precious study time if he practices swimming in the water? No! On the contrary, getting into the water validates all the hours he has spent studying about swimming. The more he actually swims, the more he will understand what he had studied in the classroom.

So it is, says Rav Mercado, with Torah study. We must spend many hours of abstract learning in the classroom and the Beit Midrash. But we also have to get into the real world to apply what we have learned. Otherwise we are like the student of swimming who never got into the water.

Of course, he understands that we are still in the young stages of our lives and that the preponderance of our time should be spent studying texts. Yet this does not preclude devoting some time to activities that help us "get our feet wet."

As I mentioned to you, I have volunteered at a shelter for the homeless. Other students have become volunteer tutors to public school students who need extra help. Others volunteer in hospitals and nursing homes. The point is that all of us who have been involved in these projects feel that we have gained enormously from the experience. We have gotten to meet people who are not part of our yeshiva world and whom we probably would never meet in the normal course of our lives. We have widened our horizons to include people of different races and religions. We have learned to interact with others; we have learned from them, and they have learned from us. We have brought the idealism and wisdom of Torah into the larger communities in which we have volunteered.

Rav Mercado teaches us that Torah is alive and dynamic. Our abstract knowledge must necessarily be deepened and fulfilled by our practical activities in the real world.

Let me point out another aspect of Rav Mercado's teachings. On the American holiday of Thanksgiving, Rav Mercado has ruled that we should omit the supplication prayers in the morning prayer service. Not only that – he also suggests that we add psalms from the Hallel at the conclusion of the morning prayers. He invites his students to join him for morning prayers on Thanksgiving. Instead of praying in the yeshiva, as we normally do every day, we attend services at Congregation Shearith Israel, the Spanish and Portuguese Synagogue on Seventieth Street and Central Park West. That historic congregation, founded in 1654, has been observing the

American Thanksgiving holiday since it was first declared by President George Washington in 1789! It was established as a day of thanksgiving for all Americans, including Jews. Our people were part of the United States since its inception. Jews fought in the Revolutionary War, distinguishing themselves by their patriotism and self-sacrifice. In Shearith Israel, Thanksgiving is marked by the omission of supplication prayers and the recitation of psalms from Hallel at the conclusion of services – just as Rav Mercado believes is appropriate.

Rav Mercado has been criticized sharply for this practice of giving religious significance to a non-Jewish holiday. The rest of the yeshiva, of course, does not acknowledge Thanksgiving in any way. The prayers are the same as on any other Thursday morning. Classes are held just as on any other Thursday. Rav Shimshon, in particular, has been highly critical of Rav Mercado's deviation from the norms of our yeshiva.

Rav Mercado, though, resists the pressures of Rav Shimshon and so many others. His argument is clear and persuasive: Thanksgiving is a day for all Americans of all religious backgrounds to give thanks to the Almighty for the many blessings He has showered on this country. We Jews certainly have good reason to be especially thankful on this day. The United States has been a haven of freedom for us. It has given us every opportunity to live according to the teachings of Torah, and has protected our rights along with those of all other Americans. Moreover, the United States has been a bulwark of strength for the State of Israel since its establishment in 1948. The question is not whether we should participate in the American Thanksgiving holiday. The question is: how can we justify ourselves if we do not? How can we justify separating ourselves from the American citizenry, of which we are an integral part? How can we not express our gratitude to God for His many kindnesses to America? How can we not be grateful to the founding fathers of this great country, who insured freedom of religion for all people, including Jews? Where would we be, where would our yeshiva be, if it were not for the rights guaranteed to us by the American Constitution?

It is fashionable in some circles to scorn American culture as something vulgar, materialistic and hedonistic. We hear that kind of talk in our yeshiva. Rav Mercado, of course, is not unaware of the problems of American culture. In fact, he understands them a lot better than others in our yeshiva, since he actually has taken the time and trouble to study and participate in American life. But he strongly objects to the simplistic preachings that depict everything about American culture in the worst light. Because people like Rav Shimshon are so intimidated by and afraid of the attractions of American culture, they demonize it so as to create as big a barrier as possible between themselves and the outside world.

Rav Mercado sees the evils in contemporary American life. He laments the breakdown in moral values. He criticizes the coarseness and gaudiness that exist in our society. He feels that the media and entertainment industries pander to the lowest and basest elements within human beings.

Yet Rav Mercado also points to the outstanding strengths of American culture. Our society values freedom, independence, hard work. The American dream has drawn millions of immigrants to these shores, people who saw America as the greatest beacon of hope and opportunity in the world. America is a land filled with compassion and charity. We have so many philanthropic organizations, self-help groups, institutions for the needy and the troubled. We give aid to other countries in need. We are the moral leader of the free world. American society encourages individuals to volunteer, to help, to contribute, to participate in government on all levels. American researchers and scientists are leaders in the advancement of human knowledge. How many lives are saved due to the medical and pharmaceutical discoveries in American laboratories? How many lives are made easier and better due to the leadership of American technology and industry?

We, members of the yeshiva community, benefit enormously from the positive qualities of American life. Rav Mercado teaches that we have an obligation to do our share to improve and strengthen society. We cannot just take the benefits of society without giving something back. He tells us that we must not be guilty of "eating the bread of shame."

The Kabbalah teaches that those who receive undeserved benefits thereby degrade themselves. They eat unearned bread, the bread of shame. We are expected to use the quality of giving, not just the quality of taking. As we give, we gain self-respect. We earn our bread.

Whereas people like Rav Shimshon see themselves as being outside – and even against – American culture, Rav Mercado sees himself as being a participating member of society who has a role to play in the shaping and unfolding of American culture. For Rav Mercado, the yeshiva is not a fortress against the outside world. Rather, it is a training ground for service to the outside world.

Yes, I agree. Rav Mercado is an unconventional Torah personality. This should not be held against him. Rather, it should be admired and respected. The yeshiva world – and our yeshiva in particular – needs religious leaders with his qualities. If he were appointed as our rosh yeshiva, it would be a tremendous step forward for our yeshiva and for our entire community.

I have heard people complain that Rav Mercado runs three to five miles every weekday morning after his prayers and before he goes to the Beit Midrash. They say that it is undignified for a Torah personality to jog in public in a sweatsuit. They argue that running is not only undignified, but it is also a waste of time that should be devoted to Torah study.

Rav Mercado, though, teaches us that it is vital for us to maintain good physical fitness. Yeshiva students do not need to be overweight, pale and physically out of shape. On the contrary, the Torah commands us to care for our bodies, to strive to be healthy and fit. Running serves this purpose for him, and a number of us have taken up the sport as well. It is not undignified to be strong, healthy, and energetic. And if he sweats in public – so do a lot of other very distinguished Americans!

Rav Mercado has explained that running – or any other concerted physical activity – is not only good for the body, but is also good for the soul. It gives a person free time to let his mind roam, to let thoughts rush freely into his head. Oddly enough, it also helps one come up with insights in Torah study. For example, it sometimes happens that you are working on a difficult problem. You think it over a dozen times, from different angles. But you can't find the solution. The more you tighten your mind to hone in on an answer, the more your mind locks itself up and prevents you from arriving at a proper conclusion. So what do you do? You forget the problem for a while. You go on to something else. And then, when you least expect it – when you are jogging, or when you are about to fall asleep at night – suddenly the answer jumps into your head with full clarity. It's like your mind needed to be left alone for a while, to mull things over on its own without your pressing it for an answer.

Rav Nachman of Bratslav once said that anyone who did not have one hour a day for himself was no man! We need time to think by ourselves, to let our minds run freely, to loosen the tensions within us. Rav Mercado has found this freedom in his daily running. Those of us who have followed his advice have been well rewarded, physically and spiritually.

What I have told you about Rav Mercado is only a fraction of what I could say about him. I think what I've said so far gives you a sense of his unusual qualities, and why he would make such an extraordinary rosh yeshiva. If you appoint him, you will be doing a great service to all of us and to generations yet to come.

I know that there are those who are afraid of giving so much prominence and authority to Rav Mercado. They shudder at the idea of having to deal with an independent, strong and innovative individual. They would rather plod along in the old, established patterns. I sincerely hope, Members of the Search Committee, that you will evaluate the candidates on their true merit, and that you will agree that it is Rav Mercado alone who can lead our yeshiva into a bright and dynamic future. Thank you for your kind consideration.

Mr. Clyde Robinson

MEMBERS OF THE SEARCH COMMITTEE: I stand before you as one of the major contributors to Yeshivas Lita. Perhaps I am the biggest donor to your yeshiva! I have been sending you one hundred thousand dollars per year the past ten years. Has anyone else been as generous to you? I very much doubt it. So I expect you to listen carefully – very carefully indeed – to what I have to say.

First, let me tell you that when I was a baby my name was Kalman Rabinowitz. That's right, Kalman Rabinowitz! It was a good, Jewish name, right? Not like Clyde Robinson. Clyde Robinson is a gentile name. I know it, and you know it. So how did Kalman Rabinowitz become Clyde Robinson, and how did Clyde Robinson become the big backer of Yeshivas Lita?

My parents arrived in New York in 1920. They came from a small town in Poland – I can't pronounce the name. It doesn't matter. It was a small town, and Jews were running away from it. It was a bad life, a hard life for Jews there. My parents got married there, and then decided to get away to America. So they got here. They had no money.

They found an apartment in a tenement building downtown, on the Lower East Side, on Eldridge Street. My father started off as a peddler of ladies' purses, leather gloves, belts – all kinds of things made out of leather. Why leather goods? He had an uncle who owned a factory that produced leather goods. So why didn't the uncle hire him to work in his factory? The uncle believed that the future depended on good distribution, so he got my father to be a distributor – by vending wares on the streets of the Lower East Side. Was that nice? Who are we to judge? Business is business. That uncle did fine for himself. When all is said and done, he gave my father a chance to make a living. My father had no money, no skills, no knowledge of English. So that uncle wasn't such a bad fellow. No, he was just fine.

Soon enough, my mother got pregnant and I was born. I was a large baby, too large for my little mother to handle. My birth tore her apart, and she died soon after. Did she have good doctors? The answer is she didn't have any doctors. Doctors cost money, and my parents had none to spare for doctors. An old woman acted as midwife when I was born. Did she know what she was doing? I can't say. I can only say that my mother died and I lived. You figure it out. I can't.

So there was my father, stuck with an infant baby. How was he to take care of me? He had to spend long hours peddling. He had no money to hire fancy nurses. His uncle – the one with the leather goods factory – offered to pay the cost of an old lady to look after me. So that's how it was. That was the beginning of Kalman Rabinowitz's life.

Somehow or other, my father managed to make progress. He started making money, and within a year or so he was paying the old lady on his own. His uncle was glad to see my father getting ahead.

When I was five, my father enrolled me in kindergarten in the nearby public school. He would pick me up every day at noon, when kindergarten was over. I would then stay with him at his cart for the rest of the day. So I learned about being a salesman starting at age five. That's a good age to start learning business, right? I used to eat lunch and dinner with my father, usually at the cart. My father didn't have the money or the leisure to take time off to eat at a restaurant. But we managed just fine.

When I was in first grade, school didn't end until three in the afternoon. So my father would pick me up then, and off we would go to our work. I loved to be with my father and I loved the smell of leather goods. We were out there on the street, rain or shine, hot or cold. By the time I was in second grade, my father had done well enough to open a small shop in a rented store on Orchard Street. Now we felt we were princes. We could eat inside. We didn't have to eat on the street like before. We could stay warm in the winter and dry in the rain. Life indoors was a big move up for us.

The years passed that way. Every day after school, I went to my father's store and spent the rest of the day with him. He closed the store at eight p.m., and then we would go home. Sometimes he would treat me to a cup of Italian ices, or a pretzel, or a pickle. Those were good times, very good times, for Kalman Rabinowitz.

My father, when he was in Poland, was a pretty religious man. He kept the laws and customs of the Torah. So did my mother. When they came to New York, they found that it would be easier for them if they gave up some of the old strict laws. America was different. A lot of Jews didn't keep the Sabbath any more.

My father kept his peddler's cart open on the Sabbath. When he opened his store, it too was kept open on the Sabbath. Even though I was just a child, and I didn't know much about the Sabbath on my own, my father kept apologizing to me and explaining his reasons for staying open on the Sabbath. He shed many tears each Saturday. He wished he could have kept the Sabbath properly, but the demands of making a living were too great. He couldn't afford the luxury of closing on Saturdays. He hoped that one day he would be rich enough to be able to close on Saturdays. Then he would resume being a good Jew, faithful to his religious upbringing.

My father enrolled me in a Hebrew school at one of the downtown synagogues. It had classes on Sunday mornings and on weekdays after school. I never went on weekdays, since I went to my father's store instead. Most Sundays, I also skipped Hebrew school so I could be with my father at his store. I wasn't a budding rabbi, was I? I wasn't much of anything when it came to being a Jew. I didn't have time, I didn't have interest. All I learned, I learned from my father. And mostly, I learned about crying for having to work on the Sabbath.

When I was nine years old, my father finally decided to remarry. He fell in love with one of his regular customers at the store. He figured that anyone who liked leather goods as much as she did would probably be a good wife for him. And she was. She was also nice to me.

My father didn't have good luck with his wives. They died young. So this second wife – suddenly and without warning – just died, after about a year of marriage. That was it. My father grieved bitterly. He blamed himself for the deaths of his two wives. They both died, he thought, as a punishment for his sin of keeping his business open on Saturdays. It was God's way of telling him he was doing wrong.

Instead of closing the store on the Sabbath, my father kept it open as usual – but he cried a lot more on Saturdays. He knew in his heart and soul he was doing wrong, but he could not stop. Business was too brisk on Saturdays. Don't worry, he would tell me, when we had enough money, we would surely close on Saturdays.

That day never came. When I was fourteen, my father had a heart attack and dropped dead – in the store, on the Sabbath. He certainly would have interpreted his death as just punishment for his desecration of the Sabbath over the years. I interpreted it as a vast calamity that punished me, not him. He was happily in heaven, but I was still here on earth, fourteen years old and all alone.

My father's uncle maintained the lease on my father's store, and I simply dropped out of school to run the business. I actually did very well. But I never cried on the Sabbath. My father cried because he remembered the holiness of the Sabbath as he had experienced it with his family in Poland. I, though, was a born New Yorker. I never saw the Sabbath observed and did not know what its holiness was, and did not miss it.

I felt that my father would want me to recite the *kaddish* in his memory during the year after his death. The problem was that I did not know any Hebrew and had never learned how to pray. I had rarely been inside a synagogue, and knew almost nothing about synagogue ritual. My father's uncle, with whom I discussed my dilemma, told me to visit Rav Leibel Grossman at Yeshivas Lita. Rav

Leibel was an acquaintance of my uncle going back to the old country. Rav Leibel would help me. If my uncle said this, could I refuse? So I went to see Rav Leibel. What else could I do?

Rav Leibel was very kind to me. He had one of the yeshiva students tutor me in Hebrew reading. I soon learned how to recite the *kaddish*. I also learned how to lay *tefillin* and eventually became familiar enough with the prayer services to follow them, more or less. Rav Leibel tried to influence me to become more observant of our religious traditions. For a short while, I actually closed the store on Saturdays. Do you hear what I'm saying? I closed the store on Saturdays, something my father had never done but always said he wanted to do.

After the year of mourning was completed, though, I quickly relapsed to my old ways. I stopped praying. I stopped laying *tefillin*. I opened the store on Saturdays. I never felt guilty about these things. I had grown up without them and did not appreciate what they meant.

Well, the years passed, and I prospered. When I was twenty-one, I had saved enough money to enable me to rent a much larger store in the heart of midtown Manhattan, on Fifth Avenue between Forty-fourth and Forty-fifth streets. Before I opened that store, I thought about what I should name it. Our old store was called after my father's name, "Morris Rabinowitz's Fine Leather Goods." I did not want to name the new store after my father, who was dead and gone. I wanted to name the store after myself. But I'll tell you frankly: I was embarrassed. Embarrassed? Me, embarrassed? Yes, yes, I was very embarrassed. Why? Because I was afraid that my name sounded too Jewish! How could I open a new, fashionable store in mid-town Manhattan on Fifth Avenue and give it such an old-fashioned Jewish name like Kalman Rabinowitz?

So I decided to name the store "Clyde Robinson's Fine Leather Goods." And then I named myself after my store. I became Clyde Robinson. Kalman Rabinowitz was no more, and Clyde Robinson was now on the scene. Clyde Robinson! Now that was a name that one could be proud of, don't you think? Clyde Robinson!

My move to Fifth Avenue was a tremendous success. The store attracted a wealthy clientele and I could mark up prices as high as I wanted. I handled only top-quality merchandise, and my customers were happy and eager to spend their money. Within a year or so, I had fallen in love with one of my customers, and I asked her to marry me. What nerve, right? What did I have to lose? I was in love with her, so why shouldn't I ask? Well, sure enough, she said yes! We hardly knew each other, except as salesman and customer, but now we were engaged to be married.

She was Jewish but knew as little about Judaism as I did. Her parents were members of a Reform temple, and we were married there by a rabbi who seemed to know even less Hebrew than I did. So it was. We were married, we moved into an apartment on Park Avenue and Seventy-eighth street, and we were enjoying living the American success story. Business was booming. I opened up several branch stores in other Manhattan locations, then opened another store in Brooklyn, several others in Long Island, and another in Westchester. Eventually, I built a chain of ninety-one stores throughout New York, New Jersey and Connecticut. I was raking in money at a phenomenal rate. Oy, Morris Rabinowitz, my beloved father! You would have been so proud, you would have been so proud. Every one of my ninety-one stores stayed open on

Saturdays. Every one, do you hear me? They remained open for business on the Sabbath. And they still do, to this day. Think about that! A good percentage of the money I donate to this yeshiva is money I make doing business on Saturdays. Is that kosher? Look, money is money. The yeshiva doesn't ask me when I earn it, as long as I give it!

In due course, my wife and I had three children, two boys and a girl. We gave them every advantage. Why not? We could well afford it. We sent them to the fanciest private schools, the most expensive summer camps. We dressed them in the finest clothes. We gave them everything money could buy and anything they could want. We took much pride in them. The grandchildren of Morris Rabinowitz, the children of Clyde Robinson!

The years passed. Our eldest son graduated from Harvard Law School, got a job in a prestigious law firm, and married a high-society Protestant woman. Look, he was not a religious Jew and she was not a religious Protestant. They were just plain young Americans for whom religion meant very little. My wife and I shouldn't have been surprised or upset. After all, we did not observe Jewish rituals at home. My stores were all open on the Sabbath. My children did not receive any formal Jewish education. Why should we have assumed that they would marry Jews, live Jewish lives, and stay tied to the Jewish community? I don't know why we supposed these things. But we did! We surely did! We were brokenhearted that our son had married someone non-Jewish. It was the end of the Jewish line for him. Our grandchildren through him would be real Robinsons, not counterfeit Rabinowitzes!

My wife and I decided to try to influence our two other children, hoping that it was not too late to keep them tied to the Jewish people. But it was too late. Do you hear what I am saying about my own children? It was already too late! They were grown up. They had their friends. One was attending Princeton, the other was at Barnard. We had raised them as though they were non-Jews, and they were living as though they were non-Jews. In short order, both of them also married non-Jewish mates. And that was that. Morris Rabinowitz, the little Jewish peddler from the Lower East Side who kept his business open on the Sabbath, will have no great-grandchildren who are living as Jews. Clyde Robinson, the successful leather goods man, the man who was ashamed to put the name Rabinowitz on his store – Clyde Robinson is the last in his Jewish line. That is the end of the Jewish adventure for our family. I am the last one. After all these centuries of Jewish Rabinowitzes in our family, there will be none left in the next generation.

In contemplating what had happened to my family, I had a life crisis. I asked myself: what was I put in the world to accomplish? Why had I failed in the elementary responsibility of every Jew to pass on the Jewish tradition to the next generation? You see, even though I was Clyde Robinson on the outside, I was still Kalman Rabinowitz on the inside. My father did not keep the Sabbath, and he cried about it. I did not keep the Sabbath and did not cry about it, but I remember a father who cried. And my children? My children have a father who does business on the Sabbath and who does not cry, but they never saw their grandfather cry on Saturdays. They have no memory, not even a faint one, that makes them understand that the Sabbath is a holy day.

My wife and I cried to each other. We never cried in front of the children or grandchildren. It would have been a waste. We pretended that everything was just fine. We saw our children and grandchildren often – and still do! And to an outsider, everything looks wonderful, happy, the American dream story. We are rich, we live well, we have prestige, our new generation is beautiful and brilliant. All is well, all is well.

But inside of Clyde Robinson, little Kalman Rabinowitz cries. And inside little Kalman Rabinowitz, Morris Rabinowitz mourns. Was this what he expected when he left Poland to come to America? Did he expect his family to disappear as Jews? Did he expect his little Kalman to die one day without having anyone to recite *kaddish* over him?

Seeing my great distress, my wife asked me if I thought I should discuss these things with a rabbi. Perhaps a rabbi could help me in some way. A rabbi? How could I show my face in front of a rabbi? I was a bad Jew, a failure as a Jew. Still, my wife persisted. I remembered how I had gone to Yeshivas Lita after my father had died, and how Rav Leibel had helped me.

So I came to Yeshivas Lita again. By this time, Rav Leibel had already died. The rosh yeshiva was Rav Yosef Grossman. Rav Yosef was kind to give me some of his precious time. I cried my heart out, I told him everything, I confessed my sins. He told me: "Maimonides states that a person who truly wishes to repent should change his name. Would you be willing to change your name back to Kalman Rabinowitz?" I thought for a moment. I felt my head bursting. Then I said, "Rav Yosef, I am no more Kalman Rabinowitz. I am Clyde Robinson. With that name I have lived and with that name I will die." So Rav Yosef realized right away that I was not coming with the sincere intention of changing my ways. Not at all. I was going to go on living as I always had lived. I was going to keep my stores open on Saturday. I was going to eat forbidden food. I was not going to pray, and not going to attend synagogue. I was not going to cut off my children or my non-Jewish grandchildren. I wanted to keep things as they were. So what did I want from the rabbi? I wanted him to tell me that I'm a good Jew in spite of all these things. I wanted him to accept me and say that God loves me in spite of my many sins. I wanted him to make me feel better.

Rav Yosef was a wise man. He knew my inner thoughts and feelings. He knew that I was not a genuine penitent. He also knew that he could do nothing at all about my children and grandchildren. They were lost!

Rav Yosef asked: "You are not willing to change your name, but are you willing to change your ways? Maimonides states that one of the rules of repentance is that one should change his deeds. Will you close your stores on the Sabbath?" I answered, as he knew I would, "No, Rabbi, I am not going to change my ways. It is far too late for that. My stores will remain open on Saturdays."

And then Rav Yosef said: "According to Maimonides, a penitent person must increase charitable giving. By sharing one's wealth, one demonstrates that this wealth is not really his – it belongs to God. God has given you rights as custodian of property and wealth, but you are not the true absolute owner. The Almighty owns the universe and all that is in it. Giving charity is a way of sharing with others, helping others. It can help change lives for the good. It has many and far-reaching consequences. Will you increase your charitable giving?"

I looked Rav Yosef in the eye, with a great sense of relief and inner joy: "Yes, Rav Yosef, this is something I can do. I am very wealthy. I can afford to give a lot of charity. I already do give charity, but I certainly can give much more. I will do this."

Rav Yosef then explained to me that I should give as much as I could to Torah institutions. In this way, my money could help ensure the future generations of the Jewish people. My own children and grandchildren are lost, but at least I can help save and support the children and grandchildren of others. The future of the Jewish people belongs only to those who study and observe Torah. Everyone else will be lost. The more people study and observe Torah, the greater will be the future of the Jewish people.

So I accepted then and there to become a major contributor to Yeshivas Lita. Rav Yosef never asked me to give specifically to this yeshiva. He told me that I should support any yeshiva I chose. But I felt I owed thanks to him, and I wanted to support his yeshiva.

Rav Yosef told me: "If you are going to contribute a large sum to our yeshiva, then we should put up a plaque in your honor. In this way, your name will be eternally linked to our yeshiva, to Torah study. The students who study in our Beis Medrash will see your name, and you will become part of their consciousness."

At first, this idea appealed to me. But what name would I put on the plaque? Clyde Robinson? I would be ashamed to have that name in the Beis Medrash. Kalman Rabinowitz? I am not Kalman Rabinowitz any longer. In any case, Kalman Rabinowitz was a great failure as a Jew. So I told Rav Yosef: "I will contribute one hundred thousand dollars a year for as long as I can do so, on condition that the yeshiva put a large, handsome plaque in the Beis Medrash which should say: 'In memory of Morris Rabinowitz, a man who remembered the Sabbath.' Will you do this?"

Rav Yosef agreed. We shook hands. I wrote out a check right then and there. The plaque was put up a few months later. I went on my way, Rav Yosef went on his way. Our lives had intersected. Our lives were changed. I was happier in my heart that I was doing something for the future of the Jewish people. Rav Yosef was happy that he had a good new source of income to support the yeshiva.

Now do you understand how Clyde Robinson came to be a supporter of Yeshivas Lita? Now do you understand the meaning of the plaque in the Beis Medrash in memory of Morris Rabinowitz?

So what does this long speech have to do with choosing a new rosh yeshiva? To me, it means a lot. I'll tell you why.

I contribute a lot to Yeshivas Lita, right? I give the money largely because Rav Yosef helped me in a time of personal crisis. I owe him something. I want his son to succeed him. I want Rav Shimshon to be the next rosh yeshiva. I believe that things like this should stay in the family. My loyalty to Rav Yosef makes me want to be loyal to Rav Shimshon, his son. It would seem simple enough. Does this make sense to you?

I want Rav Shimshon for another reason. As I grow older, I see how far away from true Judaism I am. My father didn't have the wherewithal to teach me Torah. I grew up in deep ignorance of the holy writings of our people. As an adult, I made no effort to learn Torah or to observe our laws and customs. I see now, as clear as day, that people like me are not the future of the Jewish people. We are the lost ones. We are the ones who cut off our children from their Jewish roots. We are the ones who no longer have Jewish names, who keep few Jewish practices, who keep our businesses open on the Sabbath. We are frauds as Jews. We have never been willing to face up to the challenge of living our lives according to the rules of Torah. No, we are rich and successful and do things our way. We don't want to be told what is right and what is wrong. We are rich and successful, and that is enough for us.

We are the lost ones. We have sold our souls, knowingly or unknowingly, to our evil inclinations. We do what we want, and we still want to be accepted as being good Jews. But the truth is we are not very good at all. By violating the laws and traditions of the Torah, we not only cut ourselves off from Torah, but we cut off our children. They grow up like non-Jews. We are lost, they are lost!

So I support Yeshivas Lita because it represents everything I am not. It is a place of Torah study. It is otherworldly. It is rigorously faithful to the laws and customs of Judaism, and it makes no compromises with the outside world.

My payments to the yeshiva are, in a sense, guilt money. Since I have not lived up to the standards of the Torah in my personal life, I can at least pay money to assuage my guilt feelings. I can feel part of the Torah enterprise, even when I desecrate the Sabbath and eat forbidden foods. My own children and grandchildren are lost to Judaism, but through my money, I can buy some merit in helping support new generations of Jews.

I want Rav Shimshon as rosh yeshiva because I know he will keep things as they are. He will keep Yeshivas Lita's atmosphere as though it were a yeshiva in a shtetl in Poland. He will keep it rooted to the old world, to the old ways, to the old traditions. He will keep it so that none of the students will ever change their names to make them sound more like the names of the gentiles.

Members of the Search Committee, listen to me well. I give you a lot of money, and can give a lot more. But I expect something back for my money. I expect things to stay the same. I am buying the past. I am buying the old days and the old ways. I don't want things to change here. I don't want things to change here at all.

Mrs. Esther Neuhaus

MEMBERS OF THE SEARCH COMMITTEE: Thank you for your invitation to appear before you this evening. As you know, I am one of the major financial backers of Yeshivat Lita. My husband, of blessed memory, studied many years in the yeshiva, so our family has a long and deep connection with this institution.

I was born in 1921 (no, I am not embarrassed to admit my age), the second of seven children born to my parents, of blessed memory. My parents were both born in New York, but their parents had come here from Frankfurt. Our family lived in a brownstone building on the upper West Side of Manhattan. My father was in the diamond business, and he did very, very well financially. Both my father and mother were deeply religious, and our house was characterized by rigorous observance of the laws and customs of the Torah according to the teachings of the great rabbis of Germany. My mother was part of the Hildesheimer family, and my father's family included Rabbi Samson Raphael Hirsch in its family tree. So we were the top of the line when it came to *yichus* among the Orthodox Jews from Germany.

I – and my brothers and sisters – attended Orthodox schools from elementary school through high school. When I was eighteen, and about to graduate from high school, my parents decided it was time to find a *shidduch* for me. I was a religious girl from a good family, with a father who was wealthy, and I was pretty, too! So what else could a potential bridegroom want?

My parents wished to find a yeshiva student for me, preferably one from a German-Jewish family background. My father met with Rav Leibel Grossman, the rosh yeshiva, who had just recently opened Yeshivat Lita. He told Rav Leibel about me and about our family, and he told Rav Leibel what he would like in terms of a prospective groom.

Rav Leibel was quick to come up with the appropriate candidate, a young man by the name of Isaac Neuhaus. Isaac was a quiet, diligent student. His family had recently arrived in America from Germany. They saw the writing on the wall in Germany with the ascendancy of Hitler. They knew there was no future for Jews there, so they packed their bags and fled.

Isaac spoke English with a thick German accent. He was intelligent, reasonably good-looking, came from a nice family. So the match was made.

My father, being a wealthy man, told Rav Leibel that he would support Isaac and me for as long as Isaac wished to remain in the yeshiva. Then Isaac could join the family business. Rav Leibel could not have been more pleased.

When Isaac and I first met, we already knew that our marriage had been arranged. The meeting was smooth and comfortable all the same. I did most of the talking, since Isaac was inordinately shy. He also was ashamed of his poor mastery of English. We met a few more times before our wedding. I never gave the matter a second thought. If my father was satisfied that Isaac would make a good husband for me, then I was content to go along with that decision. Isaac and I were married in the Waldorf Astoria Hotel, and we settled in an apartment on the upper West Side, not far from the home of my parents.

We had a nice, pleasant marriage. Isaac spent most of his time at the yeshiva during the early years of our marriage. When he returned home, he often did not know what to talk about with me. He only knew how to discuss issues in the Talmud and in Jewish law. He assumed that I would be unable to understand these topics. But I had received a fine Torah education and loved to study on my own. So I gradually won his confidence and we discussed various topics he was studying at the yeshiva.

Over the years we had seven children, four daughters and three sons. All of our sons studied at Yeshivat Lita, and all of our daughters married young men who were students here. Currently, two of our grandsons are students of the yeshiva, and we hope our other grandsons will also study here once they are old enough. I don't know if there are any other families that have had so many of their members as students of Yeshivat Lita. I say this to underscore how important this yeshiva is to us.

Several years after my marriage, my father asked Isaac if he would like to start learning the jewelry business. Isaac said he needed more time at the yeshiva, and my father agreed. He supported us generously, and was a patient man. A year, two years went by, and still Isaac said he was not ready to leave the yeshiva. I tried, in a gentle but firm way, to convince Isaac that it was time that he started to support our growing family, that we could not depend on my father forever. Isaac's response was, "But why not?" He was content to live off of my father's labor. To Isaac, studying in the yeshiva was his job.

Let me tell you something about my father. He loved his business. He was a magnificent salesman. He could sense exactly what his customers wanted, what they could afford, what would make them happy. He used to say that the diamonds spoke to him. When a young couple came to the store to buy an engagement ring, my father could "hear" one of the diamonds say: I am the right one for them, not too big, not too expensive. They'll like me. When a wealthy matron came into the store, my father could "hear" a gold brooch, studded with the finest diamonds, say: I am the one for her. She has good taste. She wants to show her wealth, but in an understated way. I'm the one for her. When an old man came in with a young wife, my father could "hear" a five or six carat diamond say: I'm the one for them. They want a big, gaudy stone. He wants to prove how rich he is, and she wants to show off how smart she was to have married a rich old man.

It was not that my father could really hear the jewels speak. He was such a good judge of people that he could tell almost instantly what they would want. He listened to his customers, he observed their expressions and gestures and mannerisms. He used to say that he didn't sell jewelry; customers merely found what they wanted to buy. He was a true master, and the proof was that he had a large group of faithful customers and he made a handsome income.

He thought that Isaac could learn the business from him. My father wanted to expand the business by opening other branches.

He wanted to put Isaac in charge of one of these branches, and others of our family in charge of other branches. Isaac was not receptive. He did not want to work in business. He wanted to stay in the yeshiva.

My father went to the yeshiva and had a long talk with Rav Yosef. Rav Yosef then told Isaac that the time had come for him to leave the yeshiva and go to work for his father-in-law. So Isaac had no choice. He started to work for my father.

Unfortunately, the diamonds never spoke to Isaac. He never got a feel for the business. My father decided not to put Isaac in charge of a branch of the store. For many years, Isaac simply spent five or six hours a day at my father's store. Mostly, he sat in a back room studying Talmud.

When it came time for us to put our own seven children through school, my father paid all the tuition bills. I was embarrassed by this, but Isaac was not. When our sons became students at Yeshivat Lita, my father paid the costs involved. When our daughters married yeshiva students, my father supported them. When our sons got married, my father also helped support them. Now let me ask you something. My parents had seven children, fifty grandchildren, and a growing number of great-grandchildren. Who was supporting all these souls? Who was paying all the bills while the men studied in yeshiva or proved to be ineffectual workers? One person: my father!

My father, of course, never complained. As long as his jewels kept talking to him, as long as he kept earning a good living, he could handle everything. But even he realized that there was a limit. He was getting older. He wanted to spend fewer hours at work, not more. Every time a new baby was born in our family, my father knew that he would have to defer his retirement a bit longer.

At last, he came up with an idea. He set up a trust fund for each of his seven children. He put a lot of money into each of these funds and told us that we were now on our own. He had provided for us and our families for many years, and he had set up generous trust funds for us. It was now up to us to earn our own income and pay our own bills. This was certainly not an unreasonable request.

But Isaac took it very badly. He realized that even a large trust fund would run out unless it was replenished. He had no desire to work and no aptitude for the jewelry business. Isaac sat and learned Talmud all day. It was up to me to worry about finances.

By that time, all of our seven children were married. I met with each of them and told them the new facts of life. My father's trust funds would provide a good income for them, but not nearly enough to support themselves and their growing families. They had to start thinking about earning their own incomes.

I began working in my father's store, and soon found that I also had the knack of hearing the diamonds. I worked longer hours so that my father could take more time off. I soon took over the store entirely, and I was making a terrific income. I did not wish to carry on my father's practice of supporting the whole family. I had told my children that they had to earn their own ways, and they did so. Little by little, they reorganized their lives. The men found jobs, and so did the women! Eventually, I set up a family charitable foundation and appointed my children as trustees. That fund grew substantially, and continues to be a major source for our charitable giving. As I have grown older, I have turned over some of the management of the foundation to my children. This foundation provides generous contributions to Yeshivat Lita.

Things turned out well for our family. We grew and prospered, and all of our children are self-supporting. As you know, this is not true of many families in the yeshiva community. My father, may his memory be blessed, put our family on a solid financial foundation. I saw to it that our children understood their own financial responsibilities. Many families do not have as wealthy or generous a patron as my father, and many families do not have children who are willing or able to undertake the support of themselves and their own families.

Consider this fairly common scenario. A couple has eight children. Those eight children each have eight children. And those children all have eight children. That comes to five hundred and twelve children, grandchildren and great-grandchildren. (May the Almighty bless them and multiply their numbers!) If all of these descendants devote themselves to Torah study, who is going to pay their bills? We all know families where the financial situation has grown dire. We all know cases of parents who do not have enough money to marry off their daughters to yeshiva men who expect to be supported while they study Torah.

So let me say this: I have a serious grievance with Yeshivat Lita. The yeshiva is training its students to become financially dependent and helpless, like my own husband Isaac. It is participating in a financial bubble, a bubble that inevitably will explode some day – probably sooner than later. The yeshiva needs to train its students in Torah, but also make them understand that they will have to earn livings on their own. I am afraid that the majority of the rebbeim are happy with the current system, or do not fully realize the imminent dangers. They are not sympathetic enough to the plight of religious families that do not have the funds to support five hundred and twelve members!

I believe there is only one teacher in the yeshiva who has fearlessly addressed this problem: Rav David Mercado. My grandsons are students of his, and he has had a powerful impact on them and their fellow students. Rav Mercado imbues them with a sense of self-respect and commitment, reminding them that it is nobler to earn one's own bread than to take from charity. This is the kind of voice the yeshiva needs. This is the type of teacher who needs to have greater power and influence. Rav Mercado, it seems to me, is our best hope for the future.

Aside from teaching his students to be responsible for themselves, he imbues them with the feeling that they are part of society. They benefit from the world, and they are obligated in turn to do things for the benefit of the world. They must be productive, helpful, concerned citizens. I need not tell you, Members of the Search Committee, how important it is for each person to carry his own weight in society. You all do this, I do this, my children, thank Heaven, do this. The students in the yeshiva need a leader who gives them proper guidance on this issue. Rav Mercado is the one who can best serve this role.

Let me mention another problem I have with our yeshiva. As I mentioned to you, our family is of German-Jewish background. We have distinctive customs and traditions. In Yeshivat Lita, though, it is as though Jews never lived in Germany. Our customs count for nothing, our rabbis and sages are dismissed as though they never existed. In Yeshivat Lita, there is one way – and one way only – to express Jewish religious life. Anyone who comes from a different background or who relies on different sages comes to feel like an outsider. To survive here, one has to give up all family traditions that are not identical to the traditions taught by the yeshiva.

Let me cite one example. When our eldest son began to study here, he immediately felt ostracized. Why? Because – as you know – we German Jews have our own distinctive way of pronouncing Hebrew. When he said his prayers with our German pronunciation, he was ridiculed. The rebbeim would not allow him to lead prayer services unless he changed his pronunciation. He could no longer say "sholaum," he had to say "sholoym." Well, our son wanted to fit in, so he abandoned the German pronunciation and adopted the yeshiva's pronunciation. Is this a tragedy? Not really! But in a certain way, it is a terrible thing. Why should any student who was raised in a perfectly valid and time-honored tradition be made to feel that something is wrong with that tradition? Why should the yeshiva tolerate only one way of doing things?

My husband's grandfather, Rav Shimon Neuhaus, was a learned rabbi in Frankfurt. When he died, he left his kiddush cup to my husband. It is a treasure for our family and a wonderful link to our past generations in Europe. My husband proudly recited kiddush each Friday night, using this family heirloom. But then, one Friday night – shortly after our son had begun his studies at Yeshivat Lita – our son told my husband that he should no longer use that kiddush cup. Why not? Because my son had learned in the yeshiva that one must recite kiddush over a larger cup, that his great-grandfather's cup was not large enough to fulfill one's obligation for kiddush. We were astounded. My husband, himself of the yeshiva world, blushed a bit, and started to put the kiddush cup away so as to replace it with a larger one. But I objected. I told my son

137

that if this kiddush cup was good enough for Rav Shimon Neuhaus of Frankfurt, it was surely good enough for us. Rav Shimon would not have used a cup unless he deemed it to be proper in size. So we kept using that cup. My son was not happy. He asked to have his own cup, a larger cup, so he could recite kiddush on his own. My husband acquiesced, much to my consternation.

This incident highlights one of the grievous problems of Yeshivat Lita. It establishes one set of rules and takes no other traditions or opinions into consideration. For this yeshiva, there is only one way. If you do not follow that way, you are wrong, or ignorant, or religiously deficient. Students learn, subtly and not so subtly, to discount their own family traditions. The yeshiva replaces the family as the arbiter of religious propriety. As German Jews with a rich and vibrant heritage, we resent this callous destruction of our past. We resent the implication that our sages did not know Torah well enough to give us proper guidance.

I discussed this issue with Rav Yosef, of blessed memory, and with Rav Shimshon, both good men. Yet, they showed no sympathy or understanding for what I was saying. They said: In our yeshiva, we do things according to our own pattern. We don't want students to do their own things. We want to mold them into one harmonious unit.

Well, this sounds like the philosophy of Sodom – the philosophy of cutting everyone into the same size, in the same mold, not appreciating or respecting legitimate diversity.

Rav Mercado, being of Turkish Sephardic background, knows exactly what I am saying. He is very sensitive to the injustices done to all of our students who come from traditions other than the one which dominates Yeshivat Lita. He has experienced, first-hand, the negative ramifications of this arrogant and narrow-minded attitude. If we are to move ahead in a more constructive fashion, then we would benefit enormously from a rosh yeshiva like Rav Mercado. We need someone in this position who truly understands the glory and the diversity of the Torah tradition.

In spite of my criticisms of some aspects of our yeshiva, I am fully dedicated to its future. Our family has produced many students for the yeshiva, and I hope that many more will attend in the future. The yeshiva offers a tremendous Torah experience and is a great institution. I think it would be a greater institution and a better place of Torah if it were under the leadership of Rav David Mercado.

For many years, our family has contributed generously to Yeshivat Lita. We are not complainers or nit-pickers. We don't like to make waves. We support the yeshiva because, by and large, we believe it is a fine and noble institution. We don't believe in throwing our weight around just because we make large donations, and we don't threaten to cut off our funds if things don't go our way. That is not our style. We believe in being constructive in a respectful and quiet manner.

I do want you to know that in recent years, the conversations in our family have grown more critical of the yeshiva's policies. Our respect for Rav Mercado has increased steadily. Right now, I would say that his presence in the yeshiva is an important factor in our loyalty to Yeshivat Lita. He gives us hope that things will improve.

His influence on our family has been wonderful. Finally, I must add that our eldest son now recites kiddush for his own family using the kiddush cup of his great-grandfather, Rav Shimon Neuhaus, of blessed memory.

Mr. Gershom Lyon

MEMBERS OF THE SEARCH COMMITTEE: As Chairman of the Board of Trustees of Yeshivat Lita, I thank you and commend you for serving on this committee. I know that you have given much time and effort to the search process.

When Rav Yosef, of blessed memory, passed away, the yeshiva community generally assumed that Rav Shimshon would step in and take his place. However, I insisted that the board assert its prerogative to appoint the new rosh yeshiva and not let things just happen by themselves. I called a special meeting of the board, and it was agreed that we would appoint a search committee. I then appointed each of you to this committee, and am grateful to you for taking on this responsibility.

This past week has been filled with gossip and rancor in our community. Although you have conducted your interviews with seriousness and discretion, people will still talk, people will give their opinions, people will complain. It has been a difficult week for all of us.

I have received calls from individuals who are furious that we are having a search process in the first place. They say that we are not competent to determine who the next rosh yeshiva should be. We are only ignorant laymen. They say that the position naturally belongs to Rav Shimshon, and that having a search committee is an affront to him and to the memory of Rav Yosef.

Let me tell you, Members of the Search Committee: I don't take such criticisms seriously. We are – you are – competent to decide who the next rosh yeshiva will be. The board hires the rosh yeshiva. The rosh yeshiva doesn't hire the board! We – you, as members of the Search Committee – have the right and the duty to select the rosh yeshiva.

Are you competent? The answer is yes. As you know, I am president of a pharmaceutical company. I hire and fire many people, including top scientists. Do I know more science than they do? Usually not. But I am still the boss. I determine what is best for my company. Naturally, things work out most successfully when there is communication and harmony between management and staff. Yet it is management that makes the decisions. Period.

You are all prominent in business and the professions. You know how to make decisions and take responsibility. That is why I chose you to serve on the Search Committee. Our yeshiva community needs to know who is in charge. The board of trustees is in charge!

For so many years, the board has been seen merely as an honorary committee whose purpose is limited to giving money and raising money for the yeshiva. When I took over as chairman of the board three years ago, I was determined to change this state of affairs. We are not lackeys! We are not rubber stamps for the rosh yeshiva! We are not going to pour money into an institution and then have no say as to how it operates! Those days are long gone. Our board has become more active and more responsible. You, Members of the Search Committee, are proof that a new day has arrived.

During this past week, you have interviewed the candidates for the position of rosh yeshiva. You have heard from their wives, colleagues, students, and from two major donors. I am sure you have a lot of information to process before you reach your decision.

I notice that you did not invite any of the local synagogue rabbis to appear before your committee. They do send us students and contributors from among the members of their congregations. It might have been a good idea to hear from them.

On the other hand, I see your point of view in this matter. The synagogue rabbis really don't matter. They lost their status and ceded their authority long ago. Twenty, thirty years ago, the synagogue rabbis were a force. We needed them. They helped build our yeshiva by raising money for us, by sending us students, by rallying the community's good will toward us. But that was long ago. Now the tide has turned. The yeshiva doesn't need them anymore. They need the yeshiva! We don't gain credibility by our association with them. They gain credibility by their association with us! Our rebbeim have more influence in the community than they do. In fact, they fall all over themselves to win a word of praise from our rebbeim. You were quite right not to waste your time with the synagogue rabbis. Their opinions make no difference to us one way or the other. Perhaps we will invite one of them to deliver an invocation at the installation of our new rosh yeshiva. That is enough of a token of respect to them.

Now, let me review with you what is to happen next. I will soon leave you to your deliberations. You should reach a decision by 1:00 p.m. I have called another special meeting of the board of trustees at that time. You will present your recommendation, and presumably the board will ratify it. There will be no announcement of the decision until after the Sabbath, on Saturday night. At that time, I will notify the two candidates of our decision.

I want you, Members of the Search Committee, to meet one more time with each of them, after the appointment has been made. I want you to have the opportunity of congratulating the winning candidate and of assuring him of your continued support and friendship. I want you to meet the losing candidate, to maintain his good will and to express your feelings of respect to him. In this way, I hope we will be able to keep the peace in our yeshiva community, and mend any fences that have been damaged during this search process.

Before I leave, I want to remind you that the decision is yours to make. Please make your choice based on who you think is genuinely the best candidate and who will be best for Yeshivat Lita.

Thank you. I look forward to seeing you again at 1:00 p.m.

Rav Shimshon Grossman

LAST NIGHT, JUST AFTER the conclusion of Shabbos, Gershom Lyon notified me of the decision of your committee and its ratification by the Board of Trustees of Yeshivas Lita. He asked me to meet with you this morning to talk things over, to strike a conciliatory note, to chart our path for the future of the yeshiva.

Let me make several points quite clear. First, as I told you at the outset of this charade, I believe this process of appointing me as rosh yeshiva was degrading and humiliating, to me and to the yeshiva. It was obvious, a foregone conclusion, that I would be appointed as rosh yeshiva. There was never any doubt about it. And now, you see, you have simply confirmed what has already been known and expected by everyone in the yeshiva community. Of course I am the new rosh yeshiva! Of course I will take over and follow in the footsteps of my father and my grandfather! Of course I will preserve the hallowed traditions of Yeshivas Lita! Even if you had wanted to choose another person to be rosh yeshiva, you could not have done it! Your decision would have been null and void! In any case, you would not have had the courage to defy me and the yeshiva community that I represent.

So what has your so-called search committee accomplished? It has not "found" a new rosh yeshiva, since the new rosh yeshiva – I, Rav Shimshon Grossman – was already here. No, you did not appoint me – I had already been appointed by destiny, by the universal expectation of the yeshiva world. Your so-called search only led to an increase of gossip and ill-will in our community. You allowed people to vent their frustrations and antagonisms in a manner that did credit to no one.

Let me tell you what I told Lyon last night. I told him that I was considering disbanding the board of trustees altogether! It has become a negative factor in the life of our yeshiva. The board was established many years ago for one purpose and one purpose only: to raise funds in support of the yeshiva. It had no other mandate. It has no other mandate today. I think that the board – and you as members of the Search Committee – have far exceeded your mandate and your authority. You have no business intruding on the inner workings of the yeshiva, plain and simple. You have been recruited to donate and to raise funds, to enable scholars to teach and study Torah. Your opinions are not needed, not welcomed, not wanted – and will not be tolerated by me as rosh yeshiva.

I am the yeshiva. I – with the other rebbeim – am the heart and soul of this institution. If we walked out, there would be no yeshiva. All of your money and all of your committees could not put the yeshiva together. No, it is we – the rosh yeshiva and the other rebbeim – who constitute the essence of the yeshiva. We are everything. You are nothing. I am sorry to have to put it to you so bluntly, but apparently you and the members of the Board of Trustees are too thickheaded to understand this reality. You need to be hit on the head with the facts, to be awakened from your arrogant and foolish delusions of grandeur.

We who study Torah day and night, we alone are the ones who understand what the Torah wants, what the spirit of the Torah teaches. Through constant intimacy with the Torah, we gain a certain intuition, an inner divine sense of what the Almighty is saying to us through His Torah. This holy intuition is granted only to those who spend years, day and night, studying Torah at its deepest levels. Only those who have reached this level of Torah wisdom have the right to voice opinions on matters relating to Torah and the Torah community. Everyone else is – frankly – ignorant, incapable of discerning right from wrong, good from bad. That is why they must depend upon and defer to the true Torah sages. Only the Torah sages can provide authentic, authoritative guidance and instruction.

The Torah alludes to the partnership between the two brothers, Zevulun and Issachar. Zevulun was a businessman. He traveled on ships, he imported and exported, he made a lot of money. On the other hand, Issachar devoted himself to Torah study in the tent of learning. Zevulun thought: If I am engaged in business all the time, how will I gain merit for Torah study? Issachar thought: If I am engaged in Torah study all the time, how will I earn a living? So the two brothers made a partnership. Zevulun agreed to divide half of his business income with Issachar, and Issachar agreed to divide half of the merit he received for Torah study with Zevulun. In this way, both would share in the rewards of each other's labors. They would be blessed in this world and in the World to Come.

This is the model of the type of relationship that is supposed to exist between those who study Torah and those who support them financially. They share reward in this world and in the World to Come.

I can assure you that Zevulun never told Issachar how to study or teach Torah. Issachar made these decisions because he alone was competent to make them. What would Zevulun, a merchant, know about the profound teachings of Torah? No, Issachar was the one who gained special intimacy with Torah, who was granted a divine Torah intuition. Moreover, Issachar had the right – and the responsibility – to give Zevulun guidance in how to run his business. Zevulun had to defer to Issachar in order to learn the laws of the Torah in matters of business. So the relationship was not reciprocal! Zevulun had always to defer to and obey Issachar because Issachar represented the Torah.

The members of the yeshiva's board are supposed to follow the model of Zevulun. In the past, thank Heaven, they were faithful to this ideal. They raised and contributed funds in a spirit of love and devotion to Torah. They asked for no honors, they wanted no privileges, they sought no authority. They supported the yeshiva because they wanted a portion of the merit of the yeshiva's Torah study. They were genuinely pious and righteous individuals who supported Torah study for its own sake.

In recent years, the high standards of the board have been severely compromised. Now we have a group of board members who want to interfere in the Torah study of the yeshiva. Instead of taking direction from the Torah scholars, they want to give direction! This is an outrage and it must be – it will be – stopped. My father, in his later years, saw the problems that were brewing with the board, but he felt that people would come to their senses on their own. He did not like battles and confrontations. He had faith that the members of the board would mend their ways. Unfortunately, my father's faith in the board members was misplaced.

I told Lyon and I am telling you: I want your resignations immediately. You have betrayed the ideals of our yeshiva. You have fomented tension and insurrection. You have abandoned the tradition of Zevulun.

Lyon told me that I should meet with you this morning to find a way of reconciling our differences. There is no point in this! There is a rift between us that is not bridgeable. I know that and you know that. I am willing to make a compromise, though. I will allow you to serve on the board of the yeshiva only if you unequivocally and openly apologize for your lapse in judgment in having participated in this search process. If you will guarantee to me that you will leave all Torah decisions to the rosh yeshiva and that you will engage only in the area of fundraising, then I can extend to you the opportunity of remaining on our board. Otherwise, I expect your prompt resignations. A yeshiva cannot operate properly if it has a divided board. I want and expect full compliance. I want unity and harmony in the true spirit of Torah.

Lyon reported to me your recommendation that I, as the new rosh yeshiva, appoint Mercado to be assistant rosh yeshiva. This recommendation is not in order. It is not accepted and will not be accepted under any circumstances. Quite the contrary. I told you right at the beginning that when I am rosh yeshiva I will dismiss Mercado from his position in our yeshiva. I have already done so!

Immediately after my conversation with Lyon last night, I called Mercado and told him that as the rosh yeshiva I was firing him, effective immediately. He knew better than to offer any resistance.

He told me he would not fight my decision and that he would leave peacefully. What else could he do? If he tried to fight my decision, he would only lose anyway. And we would have had to discredit him publicly, him and his wife! So he is content to sneak out without a whimper. That is Mercado for you, a real nothing!

I deeply resent the fact that your committee had the nerve to make such a recommendation to me. First, you have no right to interfere with the inner workings of the yeshiva. Second, Mercado has proven himself to be a troublemaker and a rabble-rouser. He is unfit to be on the staff of Yeshivas Lita. Third, I had already told you that I would dismiss him from the yeshiva, so how did you dare to suggest that I actually elevate his position in the yeshiva? What in the world were you thinking? The fact is that you obviously were not thinking at all!

Before leaving you this morning, I have one more thing to say. I realize that you have been recording the proceedings of your so-called search committee. I want those recordings delivered to me immediately. They will be destroyed. Any public record of the presentations to your committee must be obliterated. Why? Because publication of your various interviews can only do harm to our yeshiva. It will open wounds, raise questions and doubts. It will lead to increased factionalism and disunity. This cannot be tolerated.

Not only will those tapes be destroyed, but I expect that each of you will take an oath of silence on what you have heard during this past week. If any one of you starts to gossip, or leaks information to the newspapers – woe unto you! I tell you this without hesitation: you will rue the day you opened your mouth in sinful conversation. Your good reputations are very much tied to this yeshiva, and this yeshiva has the power to do you much harm. Your names will be tarnished in our yeshiva community. Your families will be ostracized and isolated. Your children will have trouble finding suitable spouses among the good families of our yeshiva. Don't think this is an empty threat. I assure you that I am dead serious. It is my duty to crush those who would undermine the peace and tranquility of our yeshiva. I expect – I demand – to receive all the recordings of the proceedings right away. Don't even think of making copies of them! And don't even think of trying to transcribe the various presentations based on your memories!

I don't want posterity to know that there was a search committee. I don't want this bad example to be discussed or remembered. I want it wiped out from the consciousness of those few individuals who have been involved in the search process and I want it to be as a blank page for all others, now and in the future.

I don't expect Mercado, weakling that he is, to go about spreading rumors about the Search Committee. He will keep his mouth shut. If he does open his mouth, he will be handled appropriately.

I am sure you understand my message. As far as I am concerned, as far as this yeshiva is concerned, there was no Search Committee, there is no Search Committee, and there will never be a Search Committee. Laymen never had, do not have, and will never have the right or the power to select the rosh yeshiva. That decision can only be made internally, by Torah sages.

In closing, I want to make clear once again that the role of laymen is exclusively in the realm of fundraising. Beyond that narrow domain, you have no rights and no responsibilities. You have no voice in the inner affairs of the yeshiva. You have no voice in all areas where Torah knowledge is required.

You have no voice, no voice at all!

Rabbi David Mercado

MEMBERS OF THE SEARCH COMMITTEE: I can't say that I am surprised by the outcome of your deliberations. I fully understand how much pressure was exerted on you, how much suffering you underwent as a result of serving on this committee. I thank you for your kind consideration. May the Almighty reward you for your good intentions.

I appreciate your having recommended that I be appointed as assistant rosh yeshiva. This was a gesture of respect that I sincerely appreciate. It indicates that members of the committee value my role in the yeshiva and want me to continue in my work here.

As you no doubt have already heard from Rav Shimshon, he is not going to accept your recommendation. Indeed, he has asked me to leave the yeshiva faculty, effective immediately.

I do not intend to enter a battle with him. Frankly, life is too short to waste on fruitless and painful controversies. I suppose I could appeal to the Board of Trustees or to a rabbinical court, but I have no intention of doing so. Rav Shimshon was chosen to be rosh yeshiva. I accept this without rancor.

It would have been startling to many people if you had selected me as rosh yeshiva. After all, my family background is not from Lita. My wife's family background is certainly not from Lita! Moreover, my educational philosophy is different from that which predominates in the yeshiva world. I am too progressive for some, too free-thinking for others, and too much of an activist for still others. But somehow, deep in my heart, I believed that this was a special moment when Yeshivat Lita would be able to break new ground. I had hoped, unrealistically, that our yeshiva community was ready to move in new directions. It was not to be. Perhaps another candidate will fare more favorably in another generation or two. In the meantime, I am afraid, much will be lost. The yeshiva will stay fixed in its old authoritarian rut, and the very real problems that exist in our community will be ignored and covered up. The isolationism will grow, and another generation of students and families will be led into the past.

On the island of Marmara, the place where my grandparents were born and raised, there is a great, unfinished palace sitting atop a hill overlooking the sea. It is known among the Jews of Marmara as the Casa del Pasha, the Pasha's house. There once was a powerful and rich official who wanted to build a palace that would impress the world, but he fell out of favor with the Sultan and ran out of money, and his palace was never completed. People see the Casa del Pasha as a monument to human vanity and folly. It is a grand example of how the tides of fortune change so unexpectedly.

I have often thought of the Casa del Pasha in another light. It is a symbol of the human drive to create something wonderful and enduring. Each of us, in our own lives, wants to build our own palace. We have dreams and aspirations that we want to fulfill. We work, we devote our time and energy, and we hope to succeed. The Casa del Pasha is a monument to human failure. It reminds us that it is rare for human beings to be able to achieve what we have dreamed for ourselves.

I had hoped that my palace would be here at Yeshivat Lita. I came here as a young man searching for truth. I was treated wonderfully by Rav Yosef and was given tremendous opportunities for studying and teaching Torah. My soul has found much satisfaction in the yeshiva.

Now it turns out that I must leave the yeshiva. It is a sad time for me and my family. I think that my departure will be a disappointment to my students. But the world goes on. The yeshiva, of course, will survive. And I will find another way to try to complete my own Casa del Pasha.

Right now, I am still in a state of disorientation. I should have foreseen that I would be ending my stay at Yeshivat Lita if Rav Shimshon were appointed rosh yeshiva. Somehow, I deluded myself into thinking that I would be able to continue here, either as rosh yeshiva or in my present position on the faculty. I did not think I would be cut off so suddenly.

My wife and I spent long hours last night evaluating our options for the future. We decided that the first thing we will do is arrange to go with our children on a trip to Turkey. We will return to the island of Marmara. We will visit the Casa del Pasha. Sultana and I have many memories in Marmara. Those memories have been a great source of sustenance to us in the past, and they will be a source of strength for us and our children in the years ahead.

Then we plan to travel to Jerusalem. I feel confident that I will find supporters who will help me to establish a new yeshiva there. I pray that the Almighty will grant me the wherewithal to build a worthy place of Torah, a place of light and truth, drawing many students and having a positive influence on society. I know that we will have many obstacles in our path before we can succeed. I have faith that such an institution is vitally needed and that it will flourish.

Members of the Search Committee: I know that your task has been difficult. You have spent many hours in your deliberations. You have listened to the presentations of a number of people. You have taken into consideration a host of factors – academic, communal, personal – before reaching your conclusion. Although I, for one, would have preferred a different outcome, the process itself was constructive and useful. It allowed you to gain insight into the workings of the yeshiva and the burning issues that confront our community.

I will soon be out of the orbit of this yeshiva. I am certain that Rav Shimshon will do his very best to cleanse the yeshiva of any vestiges of my influence. In a relatively short time, it will seem that there never was a Rabbi David Mercado at Yeshivat Lita. My tenure here will be swallowed up as though by quicksand, leaving little or no trace.

I assure you, though, that I will not disappear from the scene. My voice will be heard in Jerusalem, and the echoes – through me and my students – will even reach Yeshivat Lita in New York! Some day, this yeshiva and others like it will open their windows and their minds. The fresh air of intellectual curiosity and intellectual freedom will pierce the yeshiva's walls. A new era of Torah creativity and dynamism will begin. It will be a long and painful struggle to achieve this, and there will be frustrations and defeats along the way. But success will ultimately be achieved. The castle on the hill will ultimately be completed.

Members of the Search Committee: I ask you one favor before I leave. Please publish the transcript of the proceedings of your committee. Please do not allow this search process to be consigned to oblivion. All members of our community – and many people beyond our community – can learn much from these deliberations. I know that Rav Shimshon, and others like him, will not want these issues to be discussed in public. The conspiracy of silence and denial is powerful. The authoritarian approach that quashes open discussion and free speech is rampant.

You, Members of the Search Committee, have a voice. You have a responsibility to let the public know what issues have come before you. You have an opportunity to open minds, challenge assumptions, stimulate new ideas and new thinking. Please do not fail to take advantage of this unique opportunity. By publishing these proceedings, you will be making progress toward the building of your own palaces. You will be creating a lasting monument that can be a source of introspection and improvement for the community. You can shed new light on the issues confronting an idealistic institution dedicated to fostering spiritual values on the highest level.

Members of the Search Committee, please have these proceedings published as soon as possible. You have the opportunity of doing something important, something great. You have a voice. Please let your voice be heard within the community. You have a voice. Please don't let it be suppressed.

You have a voice!

Rabbi Dr. Marc D. Angel is Rabbi Emeritus of Congregation Shearith Israel of New York City and founder of the Institute for Jewish Ideas and Ideals. He is the author and editor of over two dozen books, and this is his first work of fiction.